Revenge Comes Twice

Mary Fulk Larson

NORTH mountain
N. FORK
OF THE
SHENANDOAH
NANETTE'S FARM
AUNT MIA'S
MYRTLE STREET
DOCK
WAREHOUSE
RAIL ROAD CROSSING
Serendipity
HERB
TEA
MILL CITY
MAIN
ED'S GAS
ELM STREET
CHURCH STREET
Sissy Lambert
HIRAM'S VAN

BILLY's
HIRAM'S COTTAGE
WALNUT HILLS
EMMA'S
BRUBAKER MANSION
OAK STREET
WALNUT HILLS STREET
ROSEMARY STREET
JAKE'S House
BARD'S NEST
LIBRARY
POLICE
STREET
HARDWARE
SPARE CHANGE 5¢
TOWN HALL
SOUTH WALNUT HILL'S STREET
KRAMER FARM
JENKIN'S Hollow
Custer's Mill
ANDE'S BAKERY
2017

REVENGE COMES TWICE
By Mary Fulk Larson
Volume 3 of the Custer's Mill Mystery Series

New Market, VA 22844

Cover photography courtesy of Dave and Jewel Yutzy, Court Manor
Cover design by Kevin Finnegan
Map Art by Debra Wilson

Printed in the United States
First edition
Library of Congress Control Number 2021915390
ISBN 9781737601609

Visit Custer's Mill Mysteries on Facebook
Or at www.custersmillmysteries.com

Other books in the Custer's Mill Mystery series:

Murder on Rosemary Street (book 1)
The Mountain's Secret (book 2)

Prologue

March, 1973

Two days before the last remaining U.S. troops pull out of Saigon

Anyone watching the military utility truck careening around blind corners on the pockmarked dirt road would have questioned the driver's sanity. The four U.S. Marines who sat in the back seat had no doubt that their whooping, hollering chauffeur had lost all traces of rationality. The men jostled and bumped into each other, struggling to stay upright as the driver alternated between whistling and trying to talk above the roar of the wind.

"How about that Hanoi Hilton closing for good, boys?" the driver shouted. "Our POWs are going home! What a great time to be a Marine." He stepped on the gas pedal and urged the rickety truck to go even faster on the straightaway.

The men didn't bother to try to answer back. They knew their driver didn't really want to know their opinion anyway. The youngest soldier mumbled under his breath, "Yeah, it's great if you have a ticket out of here." He felt sick to his stomach, and it wasn't only because of this insane driver. There were so many people waiting to leave Saigon; so many husbands and sons just like them. Probably most of them wouldn't even make it out of Vietnam. In fact, he wondered if he'd ever get back home.

The driver, engrossed in a monologue that only he could hear, didn't see the large pothole in the middle of the road. At least, he didn't see it in time. He slammed on the brakes, but not soon enough. The tires slid, jerking the metal frame of the truck off balance, flipping the vehicle with a sickening thud into the swampy marsh of an old rice paddy. For a split second, the passengers were airborne, arms and legs akimbo, and then they fell into the boggy morass.

For a moment the only sound was the hiss of the steam as it poured from the truck's engine.

The driver was the first to crawl out. He stood up slowly and flexed each of his limbs in turn, making sure they were all intact and that he could move them. His face was chalky white except for a streak of blood that ran down his left cheek.

Oh, dear God. That was bad. Really bad, he thought. Where was everybody? Should he try to wade into that mucky mess and look for them? With relief, he finally saw signs of movement in the tall, wet grass.

One by one, the soldiers emerged, soaked and muddy. The first man held out his arm and gritted his teeth as he clambered onto the roadway, his face pale. " Sir, I think the new kid's hurt. Bad hurt," he said. "Over there. And my arm's broken."

Two men hobbled to the spot in the grass where the young man lay. A large metal box rested on his ribs. His eyes were wide open. As gently as possible, they removed the box and each felt for a pulse.

They turned to the driver and shook their heads.

"You sure he's dead?" asked the driver.

The men nodded slowly.

"I'm gonna call for an ambulance and another truck to get us out of here. You men stay with him. Give him CPR or something. I'll make the call, then walk back a ways to make sure they don't miss us out here."

His stomach churned as he headed down the road. He was up for promotion. He'd better come up with a good story fast. His commanding officer would want to know the details of the accident. Or maybe it would be overlooked, given the general chaos of the U.S. troop withdrawal. He hoped so.

He felt a pang of guilt about the young soldier. The boy was so close to going home from this godawful war. And now his family would hear that knock on the door.

But everybody knew the back roads were terrible out here. The other soldiers would back him up, wouldn't they?

He needed this promotion. He intended to get it.

Saturday Afternoon

May 25, 2013

Precious Lord, take my hand. Lead me on, let me stand. I am tired; I am weak; I am worn.

Serafina Wimsey leaned back against the hard slatted bench and closed her eyes. The old wood-framed church window was propped open with a piece of slate rock, and the scent of honeysuckle drifted through the sanctuary. Two bumblebees vied for position just above the worn ledge, their incessant buzzing competing with the elderly soloist. Serafina wondered how many funerals Lula Halterman had sung for. Although she seemed to rely on the ancient pine podium for support, her voice was clear and strong. Through the storm, through the night, lead me on to the light. Serafina hoped Bessie had found a light at the end. Lord knows her life had been hard enough.

Jenkins Chapel was nearly full. A fact that surprised Serafina almost as much as Bessie insisting that her funeral service be held in a church.

Bessie didn't hold to religion. And religion didn't invite Bessie to join its ranks. Most people in the hollow left her to her herbs and potions and didn't try to save her. And Bessie didn't need saving. She was one of the most grounded people Serafina had ever known. Grounded and misunderstood.

Bessie hadn't wanted her relatives to put her obituary in the daily newspaper. "Ain't nothing them nosy busybodies need to know about me," she had told Serafina. "All's they want to do is see who my kin is so they say they're sorry I'm gone." But her nephew, Petey Blue Crawford, had insisted that the notice of her death be run in the *Custer's Mill Times.*

And so the people came—out of curiosity, out of nosiness lightly disguised as neighborliness, out of the hope of acquiring some new tidbit of information about this secretive, strange old woman.

Custer's Mill bookstore owner, Laurence George, sat near the front, one leg crossed over the other in an attempt to fit his lanky form into the small space afforded by the old church pews. He seemed lost in the music. His head swayed in time with the rhythm of the old hymn. Serafina wondered if he was thinking about the recent death of his brother, Alex. Alex's funeral had cast a much different atmosphere than this humble service. There was no way to create a peaceful memorial when violent death was involved.

Serafina glanced over at her friend, Emma Kramer, the town librarian. Was "friend" too strong a word? Certainly, they used to be friends, but now Serafina wasn't so sure. Life had turned out to be a lot more complicated than it needed to be. Throw a man in the mix and girl friendships were usually upended.

The Reverend Stephen Winston was not known for his eloquent sermons. And his funeral eulogies were even more ambiguous. His talk consisted mostly of reading lines from her obituary and relating a few recollections shared by Petey Blue. Bessie's wiry little nephew reminded

Serafina of a Chihuahua with his small frame and oversized personality. The man must be well up into his seventies, but he exuded the energy and curiosity of a much younger person. His sidekick and constant companion, Marv Holloway, was Petey's exact opposite. He was more of a basset hound, calm and loyal with a perpetually mournful look in his dark brown eyes.

Serafina, too, had many memories, but her interactions with Bessie had been mostly hands-on. They hadn't exchanged a lot of words during their long forages for mountain herbs and roots.

The entire congregation seemed to heave a collective sigh of relief when the reverend recited Psalm 23 and closed the service. The neighbors trailed back to their vehicles.

They knew little more about Bessie Crawford than they had when they had arrived at the service.

***

"I wish we could have hosted this after-funeral shindig next week," said Nanette Steele, as she set a tray of sandwiches on a wide window ledge while she adjusted a leaning candle. "We have that garden touring group coming tomorrow, and we're still not half ready for them."

"Really, Nanette?" Her longtime friend and colleague, Jane Allman, smiled at the scowling, sun-wrinkled face of the other woman. "Bessie couldn't exactly choose her moment of passing, now, could she?" Jane brushed a wisp of short, grey hair from her face. "Besides, I doubt we'll have a crowd. Bessie wasn't close to that many people. And let me take that tray over to the buffet before someone knocks it off the window sill."

"Well, the curiosity seekers will be out in full force," said Nanette. "Especially since we're hosting the funeral meal. Not to brag," she continued with every intention of bragging. "But there's not a place anywhere south of the Mason-Dixon line that can compete with our food."

"Who's crossing the Mason-Dixon line?" Marguerite White, the third owner of the Compass Rose Tearoom—recently converted to the Compass Rose Bed & Breakfast—came into the dining room, her starched, white apron catching a ray of afternoon sun.

Marguerite was tall, elegant and soft-spoken, her hair perfectly coiffed—almost the polar opposite of Nanette. Nanette preferred to be in jeans and boots, gathering eggs at her farm. She looked forward to supplying crisp lettuce from her garden, and gallons of cream from her best milk cow.

"Nanette is bragging about our food." Jane set the sandwich tray on the buffet. "She thinks we'll have a huge swarm of people show up for Bessie's funeral meal because of our cooking."

Jane's niece, Terri, shaded her eyes and looked out the window. Already the circular driveway in front of the former Brubaker mansion was filling up with vehicles. "Well, if these cars are any indication of the crowd, we'd better cut up some more vegetables, ladies. I know you want to be generous, but don't forget our fledgling business has very limited resources."

"Uh, I don't think we need to make any more food. Take a look at that." Nanette pulled back the curtain so they could see the entire parade of visitors.

Marguerite gasped. "Crockpots? They're carrying crockpots! Quick, Terri, bring out the old white plates. And put the china away."

"What?" Jane squeezed in between her two friends. "Oh my."

"Squirrel gravy on the tablecloths. I can see it now. Lard and chicken skin to clean up. Who in tarnation told them to bring food?" Sputtering and shaking her head, Nanette turned from the window and ran right into Petey Blue Crawford.

"Well, I reckoned you three could use some help with food. I told the folks at Jenkins Chapel to bring along some vittles," said Petey Blue. "Besides, not to discredit your cookin', ladies, but the bits and pieces of pie and bread you serve wouldn't fill up these mountain folks. Nosiree. They need meat and taters."

"Where d'you want me to plug this in?" came a voice from behind Petey. The ladies turned to see a small, grey-haired woman toting a large crockpot.

Nanette threw up her hands. "Over here," she said. "Why not? This outlet is as good as any."

The woman smiled and plopped the heavy crockpot on a delicate Regent's Park Victorian garden table. "Put it on low so it'll keep warm. Cold deer meat ain't worth its salt."

The crowd milled around the dining room sampling the delicate pastries. Marguerite held her breath as a young boy picked up an intricate antique figurine of a shepherdess.

"Put that down, Sam Lambert!" Kate Preston, the town police chief's eight-year-old daughter came up to the boy and took the ornate figure out of his hands. "You have jelly on your hands. Besides, I bet this thing costs a lot more money than you have around your house. Wanna go outside and climb trees?"

Kate gently returned the shepherdess to the side table and Sam followed Kate outside. Marguerite sighed with relief.

"That was a close one, wasn't it?" Chief Jake Preston gave Marguerite a quick hug. "You have quite a crowd here. Probably a different sort than you usually see."

"No doubt, Chief Preston. I'll bet Bertha would roll over in her grave if she could see this group."

"Quite possibly," agreed Jake. "But it's nice to see that Bessie had so many friends."

"Friends, or the curious at any rate. Both Bertha and Bessie had a way of stirring up curiosity around here," said Marguerite. "By the way, have you talked to Emma since she got back?"

"No, she just flew back yesterday, didn't she? Must be hard to come back to real life after touring Europe. Probably seems quiet and boring here," said Jake.

"I feel so bad that we haven't been able to help out more with the library." Marguerite brushed at an imaginary piece of lint on her apron. "But turning this place into a certified bed and breakfast has kept us hopping."

"You ladies have done an amazing job," said Jake, as he looked around the beautiful room filled with polished antique furniture and rare china from the Brubaker family collection. Marguerite sighed. "We have a garden tour coming tomorrow. I hope the crowd today doesn't mess up the place beyond repair."

Jake smiled as he surveyed the clusters of Custer's Mill friends and neighbors milling around, admiring the furnishings and enjoying the wide array of refreshments. "Kate and I can help clean up when it's over," he said. "Hey, there's Emma." His voice sounded wistful. "I saw her at the church, but I wondered if she'd be here."

"Talking about me? My ears are burning!" Emma came up to join her friends. Her long hair was pulled back into a loose bun, and she wore a trim navy blue suit with a crisp white blouse.

"Emma, you look wonderful. We're so glad to have you home! We've missed you." Marguerite gave her a quick hug. "We saw you at the funeral. But we were just saying we thought you might be too tired to attend the reception."

Jake put his arm around her shoulders and gave her a gentle squeeze. "Kate and I missed you, too, Emma."

"It's good to be missed," said Emma. "I'm definitely still feeling the effects of jet lag but excited to inflict my travelogue on you all. It was a wonderful trip. But I wanted to stop in and say "hi" before heading home to catch up on bills and laundry."

"Of course we want to hear all about it and see your pictures," Marguerite said. "I'm afraid I'll have to excuse myself right now to go help Jane replenish some of the desserts. Welcome home, dear." Marguerite hurried toward the kitchen.

"Let me know when that travelogue is ready, Emma. I'm interested in your European adventures," said Jake. He took her arm and pointed to the bow window in the parlor. "Can we talk over there for a minute, far from the madding crowd?"

"Sure, Jake." Emma followed him to the quiet spot, intrigued. "Emma," said Jake, "I was hoping you might have time to take a quick hike up to Mary's Rock with me on Tuesday morning." He paused. "We'd need to leave early, so you can get back before the library opens."

Emma hesitated for a few seconds. A hike her first week back at work? Surely he understood how tired she would be, not to mention the mound of work that had piled up in her absence. "I guess so," she said reluctantly. "How early – like at dawn? And will Kate be joining us?"

"No, we'll drop her off at Nanette's on the way. There's something I want to talk with you about. We can take some breakfast along in my backpack. I'll need to pick you up at 6:30, though."

"Whew, that is early," said Emma. "Well, okay. I'll take you up on the offer. It's a great hike for the early morning."

"Great, see you at 6:30 on Tuesday, then," said Jake.

Emma waved to the ladies as she left the reception by the kitchen door, but her mind was processing Jake's invitation. What in the world did he want to talk to her about that required an early-morning hike?

She was still thinking about Jake's behavior when she got home and kicked off her dress shoes. She unpinned her hair and shook it out as she carried the shoes up to her bedroom and changed into a sleek gray tunic and black leggings. Something different from her usual denim attire. She'd noticed this style on women in Germany and decided to purchase an outfit she saw on a manikin in a clothing store. It was one of her splurges, along with a pink and gray striped silk scarf. Her cat, Molasses, had followed her up the stairs and was rubbing against her legs non-stop. He'd missed her, too. She scooped him up and headed downstairs to the living room.

"What do you make of this, Molasses?" said Emma, draping her long legs over the arm of her favorite chair and leaning back on a large pillow. "Jake wants to ask me something. Do you have any idea what it could be?" As if to answer, the cat meowed and snuggled in Emma's lap, happy to have his owner back and all to himself.

Several brochures of snowcapped mountains, the Eiffel Tower, Big Ben and winding streets with small cafés displaying colorful awnings lay on the coffee table in front of her. She picked one up and sighed with satisfaction. The brochures would go in the scrapbook she planned to make, along with prints of the pictures she'd taken, plus her plane and train tickets. Jake had called it her adventure. It certainly had been. Emma hoped it was just the first of many to come. The freedom that came with getting outside your comfort zone and experiencing what the world had to offer was exhilarating.

Stroking her cat's soft fur, Emma allowed her imagination to wander. She knew Jake had feelings for her. He'd practically told her so. Was he ready for a more serious relationship? Was she? She hugged Molasses closer to her.

It was her desire to be married someday and have a family. She and Eric would have been married for years by now. But was she ready to be a wife and a mother? Was Jake ready to move past the grief of his wife's death? Kate was so special to Emma, and she loved the little girl.

Emma wasn't sure she could be the mother that Kate needed, or the wife that Jake deserved. The possibility of a deeper relationship made her feel both excitement and dread about the upcoming hike.

Monday Morning

May 27

Terri snapped a picture of the list of errands her aunt Jane had posted on the refrigerator, just in case she lost the piece of paper they were written on. She put her phone back into her purse. Never hurts to be double careful, she thought. She didn't want to forget any of the last-minute details the ladies had asked her to take care of. They were busy with flower arrangements and other thoughtful touches before their first guests arrived later this afternoon or evening.

She planned her itinerary. First, Glen's Market, then a quick stop at Andes Bakery to take advantage of their Memorial Day specials. In between, she'd need to stop for gas. She decided to save her errands at the nearby Bard's Nest bookstore until she was on her way back. The store was closing at noon today so she'd have to stay on schedule. Marguerite had reminded her several times to ask bookstore proprietor Laurence George for more copies of his local history book for the shelves in the entry hall. The ladies were certain that the folks on the garden tour would want to know more about the history of the places they'd visit. Terri wasn't so sure. But if it made them a few extra dollars, she was all for it.

Nanette had also asked her to pick up a book or two for Kate Preston's birthday, which was coming up. At first Terri protested. She knew nothing about children, much less children's' books. But Nanette was worried she wouldn't have time to shop, between the work at the B&B and her farm. So she'd given Terri a few ideas. Apparently, anything about animals would be a win with the child.

***

Just after 11:00, Terri made her final stop. The mirror-shine floors, highly polished bookshelves, and freshly vacuumed rugs in the front room of the Bard's Nest caught her off guard. She remembered more dust. When Alex George had forced his brother to make room for antiques, the place was filled with dust, musty air, and spider webs. Although Laurence transformed the shop back into a bookstore after Alex was killed, she imagined he would have piles of old books stacked on the ends of shelves and tattered paperbacks in cardboard boxes in the aisles. In short, she'd thought The Bard's Nest would still resemble a bird's nest rather than a clean, cozy, inviting shop that warmed her heart.

She tried not to show her surprise when Laurence greeted her in freshly pressed khakis and a light blue button-down shirt, not the moth-eaten tweeds she'd expected. To be fair, she had only seen him a few times. She found herself appreciating the business-like appearance of Laurence George.

"To what do I owe the honor, Miss Allman?" asked Laurence.

"Good afternoon, Mr. George," said Terri.

"Good afternoon. And no need for formalities. I'm just Laurence." He smiled.

"Then I'm just Terri."

"Lovely to see you, Terri. How can I help you?"

"I need a couple of things. First of all, do you have any more copies of your local history book? Marguerite wants to make sure we have enough in the mansion's entrance hall for our guests to look at."

Laurence looked pleased. "You mean the one I wrote? *Custer's Mill—The Little Town with a Big Past?* I believe I can rustle up some for you. Getting rid of a few, are you?"

"I think we're down to two," said Terri.

"Great. I believe I took five over to start with. Here they are." He handed Terri several copies of a thick paperback book.

"Thanks," said Terri. "I'm also looking for a birthday present for Miss Kate Preston, the police chief's young daughter." She walked toward a poster of a pink pig dressed in a lace apron. "I assume this is the children's section?"

"It is indeed." Laurence joined her in front of a display of picture books.

For the first time, Terri noticed how his salt and pepper hair curled over the top of his collar. He was tall and slim. His eyes were almost azure blue, and he moved through the store with the assurance of a man who knew his trade. Why, he was almost handsome, she thought with surprise. She had been attracted by Alex's charm, but she hadn't paid much attention to his older brother.

"A quarter for your thoughts," he said, breaking into her daydream.

"A quarter?"

"Inflation," he said. "A penny wouldn't get you much these days."

"Neither would a quarter," she said, smiling.

"Now what kind of book would Miss Preston enjoy?" said Laurence, pulling a few small paperbacks and stacking them on a side table. "Picture books? Chapter books? How old is she anyway?"

"I think she's turning nine," said Terri, "and I know she likes The *Secret Garden*. Also, Nanette said I couldn't go wrong with animal books.

Unfortunately, though, that's about the extent of my knowledge."

Terri spent several minutes looking over the selections that Laurence had pulled for her before she decided on a picture book about caterpillars and a chapter book that featured a girl detective.

"These should do the trick," she said. "I don't know a lot about children and their reading abilities. Seems like there's always somebody around to read to her, though."

"I've heard she's quite a favorite in town," said Laurence, "although I don't know much about children myself. They always seem like mysterious little people to me."

Terri laughed. "That's the truth."

"Need these gift-wrapped?" asked Laurence, holding the two books up.

"Seriously? You do gift wrapping?"

"Well, I don't publicize it, but yes. I can do a decent corner fold. Balloon paper okay?"

Terri looked at the stack of birthday paper Laurence had placed on the counter. "How about the insect one? I hear Kate likes bugs."

Laurence shook his head. "Another reason why I don't understand children. Why bugs?"

"No idea, Laurence. Like you said, kids are mysterious." Terri put her packages into her leather shopping bag. "Thank you so much for the help. Your store is a lot different than I had remembered."

Laurence sighed. "It's a lot different than it used to be. Before Alex transformed it into an antique store, I had held to the idea that bookstores were supposed to be musty and cluttered. You know, part of the scholarly atmosphere."

Terri nodded.

"But after Alex left…" he hesitated and continued, "after Alex was killed and I cleared out his stuff, I sort of liked the empty, clean feel of the place." He paused and looked around the store as if seeing it through Terri's eyes. "I'm trying a new, uncluttered, classic look."

"Well, I think it suits the place very well," said Terri. "It's very appealing."

"Thanks for that vote of confidence. It's much appreciated."

Terri's car was parked a half-block from the bookstore. Laurence stood in the doorway of his shop as she walked down the sidewalk. She turned and waved before setting her book purchase in the back and sliding into the driver's seat. Laurence returned the wave, a shy smile on his face.

***

Terri hummed all the way back to the B&B. She had certainly misjudged both the bookshop and the man. Laurence was a charming guy when he wasn't trying to impress anybody with his academic prowess. He was a bit older than she, but what did that matter? She wished they'd planned to talk again, maybe made a lunch date or something. Perhaps she'd give him a call. She appreciated a man who enjoyed intellectual conversations.

Monday Afternoon

May 27

The kitchen at the Compass Rose Bed & Breakfast buzzed with activity. The first guests would arrive within just a few hours.

Jane stood on a step stool, the cabinet door open in front of her. A Waterford crystal vase was on the top shelf, and she lifted it down with both hands. "I remember the rose arrangements Bertha put in this vase every summer. She has such beautiful things."

"They're your beautiful things now, Aunt Jane," Terri reminded her. "Yours and Nanette's and Marguerite's."

"I know, dear, but I can't get used to that fact," said Jane. "This is still Bertha's home to me. It's still hard to believe she willed her mansion to the three of us." She handed the vase to Terri. "These top shelves haven't been dusted in eons. We need to take everything out and do a thorough cleaning." She paused. "But not today. Our guests could be here any time between now and seven." She shut the cabinet door. "Would you see if you can find Hiram and ask him to cut a bunch of roses I can put on the sideboard?"

"Sure, Aunt Jane. I'll look for him as soon as I finish cutting up onions for tomorrow's breakfast casserole. Such a lot of chopping in this recipe."

Nanette and Marguerite appeared just as Terri placed the vase on the counter.

"How's everything going down here, Jane?" asked Nanette. "Marguerite and I made up all the beds and stocked the bathrooms with clean towels."

"Okay, I think," said Jane. "I feel like we're jumping off a cliff together, but here goes!"

At first the three friends had found it difficult to touch, let alone change or move anything in Bertha's house. In the months following Bertha's death, they had first transformed the house into a popular tearoom. And now, just a few months later, they had added a B&B with Terri as the live-in manager and financial overseer.

"Last year, I couldn't see you three as entrepreneurs. This kind of endeavor is not for the faint-of-heart, and I wasn't sure how it would all work out when you asked me to help get the tearoom started," Terri said.

"Neither could we, dear." said Marguerite. "But Brubakers cofounded Custer's Mill, and this home represents their legacy. We think Bertha would be proud of what we've done."

"I'm sure she would be, Marguerite," agreed Terri. "You've all done a marvelous job."

"If we have a few minutes, let's celebrate with some fresh peppermint tea. First leaves from the garden. I made a thermos before I came over." Nanette pulled a huge metal carafe from her tote bag. "Can you find four cups, Marguerite?"

"I believe I can rustle up a few," said Marguerite, smiling as she opened a cupboard filled with mugs and teacups of all sizes.

Reminiscing around the white enamel table had become a pleasant routine over the past months as the ladies worked together on their new business venture. Bertha's love of her garden roses and her famous tea parties were a frequent topic.

Marguerite held up her teacup and said, "To our latest venture, the Compass Rose Bed & Breakfast. And to Custer's Mill, the best place in the world!"

"Hear, hear," responded Nanette, Jane and Terri in chorus.

"I'm still amazed that our humble town has become so popular with tourists," said Nanette. "I knew local folks loved the tearoom. But that write-up in the Washington Journal really got the word out to visitors. It's made us a great little attraction to folks stopping in the Shenandoah Valley on their way to the mountains."

"Funny that the new road ended up helping us," said Marguerite. "It practically brings people right to our door."

"What a ruckus that road caused," said Jane. "They wanted to run that highway right through Main Street and tear down half of Custer's Mill in the process."

"Including our village library," said Marguerite. "I'm grateful Professor Nelson saved the day by having it declared a historic building, so they had to reroute the new road."

"Yes, it all worked out in the end," said Jane.

"The remodeling we did went a lot faster than I thought it would. I had my doubts about Marv and Petey Blue and their carpentry abilities." Nanette looked around the newly repainted room. "I have to admit they did an excellent job."

"We also have you to thank for this young lady." Jane glanced over at her niece. "Your good business sense has helped us make our dreams a reality."

"Thanks, Aunt Jane, but we've all put in some hard work," Terri said. "Speaking of hard work, I'd better get those onions chopped or we won't have a casserole to feed these guests in the morning."

"I agree," said Jane. "Break is over, ladies. We need to get back to the tasks at hand."

Jane gathered the empty cups and placed them in the sink.

Terri tied a white apron over her pale blue silk sweater and grey dress slacks. Kitchen work was messy, and she didn't want to risk ruining her outfit. She knew the sweater brought out the color of her blue eyes, one of her best features. She hoped Laurence George had noticed.

Kitchen work was not the finance career that Terri had studied for. But given her recent streak of bad luck, she was grateful to be here. And the ladies really did need her business savvy. They were dears, but not always practical as entrepreneurs.

She surveyed the pile of chopped vegetables with pleasure. Terri enjoyed precision, and the little vegetable cubes made a tidy pile on the cutting board. Her satisfaction turned to perplexity a minute later, however, when she turned on the cold tap of the water spigot. No water. She tried the hot tap and was rewarded with a thin lukewarm trickle.

Her eyes narrowed, and she turned to her aunt. "Aunt Jane," she said, "please tell me you delivered the check I gave you last month for our water bill."

"Yes, dear, I'm sure I did. Why?"

"Because it looks like our water has been turned off. There's no water."

Nanette and Marguerite both appeared in the dining room doorway at Terri's announcement.

"Oh no!" said Marguerite. "The guests will be here so soon!"

"Murphy's Law," replied Nanette in a matter-of-fact tone. "Things were going too well."

Jane looked stricken, and her chin quivered. "But I thought I…."She rushed across the room and pawed through her brown leather bag, tossing the contents haphazardly onto the kitchen table. In desperation, she turned the bag upside down and shook it. Dust and unidentified bits of debris sifted down, along with a crumpled check.

Her face drooped. "But I don't understand. It's still here. In my purse. Oh my." She put her hand over her mouth. "I guess I… oh, I can't believe I forgot to take this in!" Jane sat down heavily on a kitchen chair. "Now I've ruined everything! We can't do anything without water!"

Terri's severe look softened, and she put her arm around her aunt. It was impossible to stay angry with such a sweet-tempered woman. "We'll figure it out, Aunt Jane. Don't cry."

"Give me the check." Nanette said. "No use crying over spilled milk. I'll straighten it out. A lot of nerve they have turning off our water today. Today, with all the publicity around town about our grand opening. I have a few choice words for that new town manager of ours."

Marguerite winced as the front door slammed. "I hope she knows what she's doing," she said as she watched the rusty pickup pull out of the driveway. "I'm afraid she'll make the entire town office mad and we'll never have water."

Jane's voice was tremulous. "I feel terrible about this." She squared her shoulders and took a deep breath. "But, as Nanette would say, 'the show must go on.' I guess it's back to work, sans water, that is. We can still set up the dining room and do a final check of all the bedrooms before everyone arrives. And let's pray the water is on within a couple of hours and the guests don't come until after that."

***

The sun made a striped shadow across the blue gingham tablecloth at the most popular restaurant in Custer's Mill, the Spare Change Diner.

A dark-haired young man sat alone, his backpack at his feet. He tipped his chair back and surveyed the rustic room with interest. The regular folks who gathered for the all-day breakfast special were careful to avoid catching his eye. A stranger in their midst was a curious event, and they'd enjoy discussing it later. But for now, they shared raised eyebrows and furtive glances.

Marv and Petey Blue were among the few diners who ignored the visitor's presence even though the young man sat down at the small cafe table beside them. The two old-timers were deep in discussion about the welfare of the young chestnut grove hidden in the forest near Jenkins Hollow.

"How're we gonna take care of them trees now that Bessie's gone?" Petey pushed some scrambled eggs onto his fork with his finger. "I'm not thinkin' we'll stay in these parts much longer, Marv. And, anyhow, I hate to admit, it's gettin' harder for us to manage by ourselves out in the woods." He stuffed the eggs into his mouth and washed them down with a swig of coffee.

Marv nodded and buttered his blueberry muffin without comment.

"Who's gonna protect our seedlings?"

Marv shrugged. "Need to find someone."

Petey lowered his voice to a near-whisper. "Well, that ain't rocket science. But do we advertise that we're lookin' for someone to watch over trees that ain't ours to begin with, and are planted in the national forest?"

Marv put his finger to his lips in a warning gesture. The waitress had stopped directly beside their table and served the young man his breakfast special. She blushed scarlet as he tipped his head and thanked her. Customers as good-looking as this man were a rare treat at the diner.

"As I was sayin', Marv," said Petey after she'd walked away. "Who's gonna watch over that grove of trees? All we need is one forest ranger to spot those chestnuts and the saplings will be completely out of our hands.

The government will take 'em and claim all the credit for their health and well-being. And you and me both know the government can't be trusted. No how. No way."

Marv nodded.

"So, what do we do? We're in a pickle. Unless we want to give up our ramblin' ways and settle down, I don't see how we can protect our trees. And we need to head back over the mountain and continue our amateur investigation business. This tree situation is holding us back."

Both men looked glum, then Petey continued, "I've already got three calls from old man Wade about somebody messin' with his prize hog. He thinks it's Liza Donovan who's been feeding that pig junk. Why, Wade even found some henbane in the trough the other day. Everybody knows henbane is fatal to pigs!"

"That's right," said Marv.

"It goes without sayin' we have to get back over the mountain and do a little investigatin' before fair time. I know Liza wants her hog to win best-in-show this year. Wouldn't surprise me at all if she's not the one trying to sabotage Wade's pig."

Some minutes passed as the men continued eating their bacon, eggs and grits, deep in quiet conversation. Petey stopped mid-sentence and motioned to Marv with a nod of his head. They both looked up suspiciously at the young man who was standing beside their table. . "Excuse me, gentlemen," he said, in precise English that held more than a trace of a foreign accent. "But I gathered that you are in the market for a horticulturist, yes?"

"A what?" Petey's voice was gruff. He didn't take to foreigners. "If you mean somebody from the government, I say no sir and no way."The young man smiled. "No. No government work for me. I said 'horticulturist'. A person who studies plants. Please, allow me to introduce myself. David. David Nicolescu."He held out his hand, and several seconds elapsed before each of the older men reluctantly shook it.

"Well. Didn't know you were listenin' to our private conversation, sir." Petey leaned back in his chair. "I don't take to people eavesdroppin' on things that are none of their business. Just what did you hear? Marv, I don't recall saying we needed a hor-to-culture-ist. Do you?"

"I wasn't trying to listen in, but when I hear about plants and trees, I can't help myself. It's my love, my special interest."

"Shh. Keep yer voice down, man. Don't go blabbin' on about it. Marv, let's us and this David settle up here and take our conversation outside." Petey Blue pulled several wrinkled bills from his wallet and stood up. "Katrina," he called to the waitress who still eyed the newcomer with interest, "We're puttin' the money for our vittles on the table. Keep the change. Buy yourself some bubblegum." He sniggered at his own joke and motioned for the other two men to follow him.

The sun was bright, and the men shaded their eyes as they walked out into the warm May day.

"Now then, David, let's do us a proper introduction. I'm Petey Blue Silas Crawford and this here's my business partner and friend, Marv Holloway." The men shook hands.

"How 'bout we set over there." Petey motioned toward a green bench at the corner of the street. "Don't suppose too many folks are out and about now. Should be as good a place as any."

The men watched a young girl struggle to pedal her bike uphill toward the library. The huge, pink backpack on her handlebars wasn't helping her progress.

"Looks like young Kate Preston," said Petey. "Our town police chief's daughter," he added with a sidelong glance toward David.

The young man looked startled and Petey nodded slowly. "Just like I figured. You ain't too anxious to hear about lawmen, are you? Got something to hide, I'll wager."

David said nothing, so Petey continued. "You wouldn't be missin' one of them green cards, would you? Maybe it got lost or something?"

David stiffened. "Why do you say that? And would it bother you if I —as you say— misplaced my green card?"

Petey rubbed his hand over the stubble of his beard. "Well, I ain't one to judge folks who don't play by the letter of the law. I guess it would depend on the story you tell. You ain't no criminal, are you? You kill somebody? Are you runnin' from the law?"

David smiled. "Oh no. Nothing like that. My story is long and tragic, but I assure you, good gentlemen, I am not a violent man."

"Why were you listenin' to our conversation back in the diner?" Petey Blue waved his hand as David started to talk. "Now don't go spoutin' off about how you love gardens and roses. You very well may be a hor-to-cultureist, but I want to know the real reason your ears perked up when you heard us talking about trees."

"It's all quite simple. I'm looking for a job."

"Go on," said Petey. He leaned closer to the stranger.

"It is true. I love plants.I've worked at some large gardens in Europe and two here in the States. But I kept hearing about this beautiful valley and decided to seek work here. So that's why your conversation caught my attention." David looked apologetically at the men. "I'm so sorry if I offended you."

"Pretty story, but pardon me if I don't believe you." Petey's pointed look took in the man's old jacket, his clean but worn shoes, and his long slender hands.He raised his eyebrows. "Those hands haven't dug in the dirt. Not much anyway."

"Oh, but they have," protested David. "I wear work gloves when I work. I am also a musician, so my hands must be preserved."

Petey chuckled. "Preserved hands. If that don't beat all."

Marv shook his head at the clever wit of his friend.

"Well I don't know if I trust you, and I don't even know if I like you," Petey said, his eyes narrowing. "But Marv and me might have something that could interest you. But we ain't gonna talk about it in front of you. You stay here and Marv and me will have a confab over in my truck. If we can agree, you might have a job."

Petey and Marv walked over to the old pickup truck parked near the curb. The passenger door scraped on the sidewalk as Marv opened it. The inside was stifling hot but both men rolled down their windows only an inch or so. Petey dropped his voice to a whisper.

"Okay, Marv. Here's the thing. This man might be our answer. We needed someone to care for our trees and then he appears right before our eyes. He's foreign, though. What do you think?"

Marv shrugged. "Wonder if he can keep his mouth shut?"

"The way I've got it figured, a man who's not exactly here in a legal way's not gonna have anything to do with the authorities. You hear how he hedged around the green card question? I'll ask him again and you watch."

"I agree," said Marv. "I think there's more to him than he's sayin'."

Petey tapped his head as though a light was suddenly turned on in his brain. "I have an idea. What if I let him stay in Bessie's house for free if he looks after our trees? We'd be sorta on equal footing, both of us not exactly adhering to the law of the land, I mean. We could make a deal."

"Quid pro quo," said Marv.

"You and your Greek, Marv," said Petey, shaking his head.

"Latin," said Marv.

"Okay. Let's run our plan by him and see what he thinks. Agree, Marv?"

Marv nodded.

The men returned to David, who watched them with an amused expression.

"So, young man…David. What about that green card?"

"You want me to fill out some paperwork, yes?" David's face became tense, though he continued to smile. He pulled out a wallet and leafed through it. "I'm afraid I don't have my card with me right now."

"Hmm. Ain't that curious? Kinda figured it might be that way." Petey sat down beside David and put his hand on the young man's shoulder. "Well, it ain't the end of the world, son. We might be able to work out a deal despite the lack of paperwork. You come to us at a most fortuitous time, son.My old Aunt Bessie, she just passed away, God rest her dear soul. And as I'm her one and only heir, Lord willin' and the creek don't rise, her house will soon be mine. Mebbe you could stay there for a bit and watch over her patch of herbs and some little trees me and Marv have growing in the forest 'round there. I reckon you'll need us to drop off a few vittles before we head on over the mountain. What I'm offerin' is room and board for babysittin' our trees."

David's face relaxed. "A caretaker of plants? For food and place to stay? Wonderful! I want to study the plants of the forest in this area. Herbs are a special interest of mine. But," he paused, "what of this creek rise you speak of? Will water threaten the gardens?"

Petey Blue slapped his thigh and hooted with laughter. "It's a way of talkin," he said, once he calmed down. "A figger of speech. 'The Lord willin' and the creek don't rise' is a way of sayin' I'll get my Aunt Bessie's house unless something unexpected happens."

David smiled. "There is much I need to learn about your language."

"You ready to shake on our little deal? I think we understand each other right well." Petey and Marv held out their hands.

David's handshake was firm and decisive. "Yes, we do, sirs. I think our arrangement will work out for both of us. Thank you, again! And now, will you take me to this Aunt Bessie house? I have all my belongings with me." He pointed to his backpack and a worn violin case.

"Come on then," said Petey." Throw yer things in the back and let's be on our way. The Lord does work in mysterious ways!"

The truck rumbled and shook as it roared into life and headed off to Jenkins Hollow and the rutted, uneven lane that led to Bessie's remote cabin.

***

Petey Blue led the way as the three men broke through the thick pine forest into the clearing behind the old Crawford place. "Now Dave, we want you to understand that we're entrustin' you with the most valuable thing we have. That stand of trees back in those woods is our legacy. Me and Marv have been nursing that their American Chestnut grove for about five years now. It's our little miracle. And it's a goldmine, too."

David nodded. "I understand. Your secret will be my secret also." He ran his fingers through his curly black hair, dislodging pine needles and a stray leaf or two.

"We'll take a look at the old house now. It ain't no mansion. Don't want you to be expecting something that's not there."

David smiled. He looked at the weather-beaten boards of the old house and shrugged. "I am not accustomed to luxury and will be happy to have a warm, dry place to stay."

"It's surely not luxury, but it's comfy enough," said Petey.

A weathered rocking chair on the front porch swayed slowly in the wind, as if it could barely summon the energy to move.

Petey removed his hat and held it in both hands as he stood on the porch. "I'm used to seeing Aunt Bessie rocking in that shabby old chair," he said, his voice soft and mournful. "I declare this place seems mighty empty without her."

The pine floor creaked as the three men entered the house. A cotton rag rug in shades of blue covered most of the age-darkened boards, and a round wood stove sat in the center of the room, its iron frame cold and dusty.

"She didn't have many visitors, did she?" David pointed to two rockers on either side of the stove and a plastic lawn chair in a corner. "Few places to sit."

Petey glanced around the room as if seeing it for the first time. "No, I expect she didn't have many people out here. At least not many at a time. Most of the holler has been up here at one time or another though. Lookin' for cures for rheumatism or a bottle of love potion."

"So, she was a *drabarni*?" David looked at Petey Blue in surprise.

Petey scratched his head. "Not sure what that is."

"A shaman. Perhaps you would say a healer."

"Well, all I know is that she used the remedies the good Lord gave us. Not many folks slow down enough to find healing from nature. They'd rather take some kind of poison pill from a doctor. One of them MD's that are supposed to know everything. Well, Aunt Bessie didn't know everything, but she knew a good bit about human nature. How people behaved and what made them sick. She knew how to make 'em better too."

The group wandered into the kitchen. Glass canning jars lined the shelves around the wood-fired kitchen stove. Each container was filled with dried herbs, multi-colored grasses, and gnarled roots. None of the jars had labels.

"How'd she know what she was using? She didn't put names on anything?" David picked up a small, fluted container and inspected the white flowers inside. "Snake Root."

Again, Petey smiled. "I see you know your stuff, son. Bessie's eyes started to fail her near the end. She'd take off the lid and smell what was inside. She knowed them by their scent."

David nodded. "I would love to have that gift. That talent for knowing."

"Knowing what?" Petey looked puzzled.

"Knowing the secrets of the universe."

"Well, I wouldn't say Aunt Bessie knew all of that. Just how to soothe a sore tooth, clear up a rash. Sometimes fix a broken heart."

David sighed, his dark eyes suddenly bright with tears. "My heart is broken into a million pieces. The pieces are scattered all over the world." He made an expansive motion with his hands as if including the universe in his statement.

"Now don't take on so, boy!" Petey stepped back in mock surprise. "You're a young'un. You have plenty of time for romantical interludes."

David shook his head. "There's only one for me. I was an idiot, and now she's gone. I'm so sad."

Petey nudged Marv. "You know what that's like, buddy. Don't you?"

Marv bent over and picked at a piece of gravel embedded in the sole of his boot.

Petey continued, "Me, I never let nobody near my heart. Women are trouble with a capital "T." Nosiree. Give me a shack in the mountains and enough to eat and I'm happy. Don't need nothing else."

"You are one lucky man." David looked at Petey with admiration.

"I expect I am. Now, let me show you the rest of this place."

The back bedroom had the same sparse accommodations as the rest of the house. A single iron bed sat in the center of the room framed by two plain dressers. A small wicker chair still held Bessie's bonnet and apron.

"That bed," Petey gestured to the quilt-covered mattress, "is worth its weight in gold. Antique. That was Bessie's grandma's bed. And those dressers? Worth even more."

David whistled. "You mean that old furniture is valuable?"

Petey Blue and Marv exchanged glances. Marv nodded almost imperceptibly, and Petey Blue answered. "Yeah. And upstairs we have a lot more pieces that some collector would love to get his hands on. You need to be careful. Lock up when you leave. Don't let any strangers inside."

David looked puzzled. "You mean I'm guarding treasure? I don't know..."

"We trust you." Petey Blue placed his hand on the young man's shoulder. "and not just with the antiques. That grove of American Chestnut trees is just as important as anything we have in the house. Maybe more."

"I've heard about the chestnut blight that wiped them out in the first half of the last century." said David.

"Well, almost wiped them out. Our grove is still going strong."

David whistled. "Then you do have treasure."

"Whoowee, it looks like we got us here a man who appreciates our little miracle." Petey Blue clamped David's shoulder. "You're a perceptive man."

David frowned. "How big are your trees? When does blight set in?"

"We're not rightly sure. We know that when it does, it spreads quickly."

"You probably won't... I mean with your age..." His voice trailed off.

"Well, I believe he's sayin' we're old, Marv." Petey laughed at the young man's discomfort. "Me and Marv are well aware of our time restrictions. We've been looking for a young person to come along—someone to take an interest and want to continue watching over these trees. I tell you, seems like divine intervention that brought you here to Custer's Mill. Isn't that right Marv?"

Marv nodded.

"So, what do you say, boy? Can you handle the mission?"

David gazed around the room and nodded slowly. "I will watch over your trees and stay here until you return."

David stood in the doorway as the two men backed out of the driveway and headed down the mountain. He inched his backpack off his aching shoulders and set it on a small chair in the corner. Pushing a dusty curtain away from the kitchen window, he gazed at the breathtaking mountain view. Then he bowed his head and clenched his fists as he whispered an urgent prayer. "Let me find her. Please."

The ancient clapboard siding creaked as the wind swirled around the eaves of the old house.

Monday Evening

May 27

"They're here! The bus just pulled up." Marguerite tugged at the ties of her apron and smoothed out the imaginary wrinkles on her flowered silk skirt. "Thank God you got the town to turn our water back on, Nanette. That could have been a disaster."

Nanette sniffed. "Ridiculous town manager."

A white charter van had pulled into the circular driveway in front of the grand house, and its passengers spilled out onto the front walkway.

"Too late to turn back now," murmured Jane, as she peered over Marguerite's shoulder. "We're in this now, for better or for worse."

"Oh, for heaven's sake, Jane, we're not performing a marriage ceremony!" Nanette opened the curtain wider. The bus driver was unloading mountains of satchels and suitcases. "Good grief! With all that luggage, they must be planning to stay all summer! I'm going to find Hiram. Looks like these folks could use some help."

"Grab Terri, too, if you see her. I don't know where she went," Jane called to Nanette as the women walked to greet the visitors who gathered on the circular driveway.

"Good evening, ladies. I'm the tour group leader, Frank Wright." The tall, white-haired man moved toward the ladies with his hand extended. he swept off his hat with a flourish.

Marguerite shook the offered hand and smiled. "I'm Marguerite White. And this is my friend, Jane Allman, another owner of the Compass Rose."

"What an absolutely gorgeous place! Your brochure doesn't do it justice!" His gaze took in the old mansion, resplendent in the evening light. "A perfect picture of Greek revival elegance!"

"Yes, it was built before the Civil War by the Brubakers, a successful merchant family credited with helping to found our little town.

"I think we have some help coming," said Jane. "Looks like you might need a few more hands to get these bags into the house."

Frank bowed slightly. "Very gracious of you both. They did seem to bring a lot with them." He eyed the growing pile of luggage with dismay. "I don't know how they ever got it all into the bus!"

"Oh, and here's Terri. She's just the one who can help your group get organized," said Jane. "Terri, meet Mr. Frank Wright, the tour group leader. Frank, this is my niece, Terri Allman, our business manager."

Frank's eyes traveled up and down Terri, registering his appreciation with a cocky smile.

"Pleased to meet you, sir," said Terri. She gave his hand a brisk shake. "If you'll stop here a minute, I have all the rooms assigned and I can direct your group. Now if everybody has his or her name tags on their luggage, we should be good to go."

Frank looked doubtful. "Well, I told them to make sure they labeled their stuff, but you know how that goes. Some listen and some ignore."

Terri continued to flip through the pages of her binder, oblivious to

Frank's attempt at casual humor. "I see. Let's hope everything gets where it needs to go."

Frank looked at his watch. "I'm sure everyone would appreciate getting settled as quickly as possible. We've had a long day, starting this morning when we boarded this bus in Falls Church at 6:00 am."

"Yes, well, I'm sure we can get you settled as soon as I get everyone inside and the luggage up to their rooms. By the way, are most of these people retired? I hope the steps to the second floor won't be a problem."

"I'm sure they'll be fine, miss. They're all pretty spry. No worries, of course with young Sarah and Andy over there."

Terri narrowed her eyes. "Yes," she said slowly. "They do seem to be an anomaly. At least compared to the ages of the other group members."

Frank laughed. "I'll take that in the spirit it was offered! Yes, they are a bit different from the usual garden tour crowd. They won this trip. A perk for joining my new company—Living Healthy. Have you heard of it?"

Terri looked puzzled. "Can't say I have. I thought you were a tour director, not a business owner.

Frank laughed. "Well, let's just say I wear many hats."

"So it seems." Terri had just moved aside to let the members of the tour group enter the mansion when loud voices erupted from behind the parked tour van.

"No! I'll carry it!" Hiram was engaged in what appeared to be a fierce tug of war with a tall, elderly woman.

"No, you take that turquoise bag over there. I'll carry the leather satchel!" the woman shouted.

"Don't boss me around," said Hiram. "Be glad I'm helping to lighten your load. I'm a gardener, not a bellhop."

"You're a nuisance. I want to carry this bag. You take the other one."

"Oh, why does it matter, Isobel?" asked a chubby, white-haired woman who struggled to pull the handle out on her large suitcase. "Let the poor man help, Sister."

"He's not helping if he's being belligerent, Glenda."

"How long will the sharp-tongued woman trouble me," said Hiram, rolling his eyes.

Both Isobel and Glenda drew back. "What?" they said in unison.

"Don't let the scripture-quoting gardener get to you," Nanette said as she came from behind the bus, her arms full of travel bags. "He means well."

Hiram let go of the old leather bag and Isobel stumbled backward. "Funny way of showing it," Isobel mumbled.

"This place is beyond lovely," said a small, thin woman. She hoisted a large camera bag over her shoulder. "My name is Martha," she said to Nanette. "This would be a perfect site to do a photo shoot for a piece I'm working on. Do you think that would be okay?"

"Of course," said Nanette. "We're pretty proud of our establishment, and we like to show it off."

"Perfectly understandable," said Martha. "I'm surprised your garden isn't listed on our tour."

"We haven't gotten that far yet," said Nanette, as she watched two young people at the far end of the driveway. "They don't seem too eager to join us, Martha. Are they shy?"

Martha smiled. "I don't know what's bothering those two. They have griped and grumbled the entire trip so far. They seem to have a grudge toward everybody and everything."

"Well, to each his own," Terri said. "I'm guessing they're Sarah and Andy? They're the only two names I haven't crossed off the list."

"Yes," said Martha. "Sarah and Andy. Frank's reluctant protégées."

Nanette looked puzzled. But before she could ask questions, Martha had taken her camera out of the bag and had wandered toward a hedge of Harkness rose bushes.

"Welcome, everyone!" Marguerite paused at the top of the steps of the wide veranda and addressed the group. "You folks get settled, then we'll have refreshments for you in the parlor. And there's still a little daylight to enjoy the gardens."

***

"Look, here's a welcome tray," said Sarah, as she tossed her suitcase on the bed. "How sweet!"

"Probably poison," said her husband Andy. "Can't imagine old Wright taking us on a luxury tour without some strings attached."

"I'm really sorry you're already having a bad time," said Sarah, as she joined him by the window. "I had hoped you could forget why we're here— at least for a while. This is such a pretty house."

"Humph." Andy placed his suitcase on the bed next to Sarah's and let his gaze travel around the bright, cheery room. "I'm afraid my conscience won't let me forget. I've been taken in by that snake-oil salesman, Sarah. Every time I see him, I'm reminded how gullible I've been."

"You forget, Andy, we've both been conned by Frank Wright," said Sarah. "It was our life's savings together that we used to buy into this 'get-rich-scheme.' No use crying over spilt milk, as my dad would say." She moved closer to Andy and rested her head on his shoulder. "Can't you simply relax and enjoy the next few days?'

"Your dad would never have made such a huge mistake and if he did, he'd have enough money to cover his losses." He put his arm around Sarah and pulled her toward him. "You don't know what it's like to go without and to struggle to keep what little you have."

"Well, I know if we asked him, my father would give us money."

"That's not the point." Andy let go of his wife and moved a few steps away. "I don't want your father's money. It's my job to take care of you now, but it makes it difficult when I make such stupid mistakes. You're used to being rich and having anything you want."

"So are you saying I'm a spoiled rich girl?"

Andy walked to the window and jerked back the curtains. "It's kind of true isn't it?"

"Andy, that's not fair," said Sarah, but her husband had already stormed out, slamming the door behind him.

***

After iced tea and cucumber sandwiches, the rest of the tour group wandered out to look at the Brubaker gardens in the fading light of evening.

"The Rosemary Harkness, you say?" Glenda gently touched a velvety petal of the peach-colored rose. "That's lovely! Is that where Rosemary Street got its name?"

"Not sure." Nanette swatted at a firefly as it flew past her face. "Probably not, I don't think the roses are that old."

"Planted them in the 70s," said a raspy voice behind them. Hiram had followed the group up the path, his eyes still warily on Glenda's sister, Isobel. Hiram wasn't a gracious loser. He straightened the ragged baseball cap and pulled a stray leaf from his graying ponytail.

Nanette put her hand on Hiram's thin shoulder. "Can't understand much of what he says, but I believe Hiram here is one of the best gardeners in the country. I'd put him against old Thomas Jefferson if that man was still alive."

Hiram shifted from one foot to another, clearly not comfortable with the compliments, but not wanting to leave either.

"What a fabulous job you have," said Glenda. "I'll bet you love being around these beautiful plants all day long!"

"Speak to the earth and it shall teach thee."

"Pardon me?" Glenda gave Hiram an incredulous look.

"Oh, that's how he talks," said Nanette. "He and King James are buddies."

Hiram nodded to the group. "Gotta put my tools away." He started toward the old green garden shed.

"Is that where he lives?" Glenda pointed toward the small structure as Hiram disappeared through the door.

"No, he lives in that white cottage beside the shed. Miss Bertha left instructions in her will that Hiram was to live there as long as he wants to. He used to stay in the Green Hornet, that beat-up old van parked next to it. The cottage is a step up for him, and it's also convenient for us."

"Hey friends! Look at this!" Frank called from near the stone wall. "It's St. Fiacre!"

"St. Who?" Nanette herded the little group across the lawn to where Frank stood in front of a small statue.

"St. Fiacre. The patron saint of gardening and medicinal herbs. Usually gardens have statues of St. Francis, but he was only the patron saint of birds and animals. Poor old Fiacre gets overshadowed by the radical Francis."

"Hadn't really noticed him," said Nanette. "He must get covered by the wisteria when it's in full bloom." "Look at those jewels around his neck!" Martha lifted a small necklace from around the stone figure.

"Just rhinestones, I'm sure," said Nanette. "Bertha must have put them there. Wish they were real diamonds. I could use a few extra thousand. Well, folks, you all come on in when you're ready. I'll leave you to explore on your own.

"I think we're losing daylight," said Frank. "We'd probably better come in now too. Don't want anybody stumbling over tree roots in the dark."

"Isobel," called Glenda, "Please come join the rest of us! We're going inside now!"

Isobel had stopped by the statue of St. Fiacre. "I'll join you in a minute, sister. I am admiring the lovely irises here. Black irises."

Both Sarah and Andy were seated on the front porch swing when the others came in from the garden.

Frank appeared not to notice Andy's open hostility toward him and sat down on a padded wicker chair near the young couple. "Beautiful gardens here. Perfect setting for our tour. Good pick, isn't it?"

Andy grunted, and Sarah stood up. "It's too hot out here. I'm going back up to our room. At least it's air-conditioned."

"I think we'll go up too," said Isobel as Glenda trudged up the steps. "Come along,

"Yes, sister," said Glenda meekly.

"I think I'll take my tea out to the garden bench," said Martha. "I'd like to watch the last of the sunset."

"Well, that leaves just you and me," said Frank, motioning for Nanette to join him. "Pull up that chair and rest your weary bones."

"Wish I could," said Nanette. "But I have to get back to the farm. Horses need to be fed, eggs gathered before full-on dark. I'm getting behind in my work. Didn't get the beans planted today and they're calling for rain tomorrow."

Frank looked surprised. "Oh, I didn't know you were a farmer too."

"I pretend. Parents left me the place. I do what I can."

"Well good for you. We need more people who care about the land." Frank suddenly reached up and put his hand on top of his head. "Darned if I didn't leave my hat out in the garden. Guess I'd better go fetch it. Especially if it's going to rain tomorrow."

Frank headed toward the patch of begonias near the rock wall where he'd left his hat. On the way, he passed the statue of St. Fiacre. He chuckled when he noticed the rhinestone necklace was gone. "Just as I thought," he said.

Returning to the house, Frank carried his small bag up the grand stairway and deposited it on the floor inside his room. He walked to the large bow window and stood gazing at the shadows making stripes across the manicured lawn and intensifying the blue mountains in the distance. "Nancy, Nancy," he whispered softly. "I wish to heaven you were here seeing this with me."

Several minutes elapsed as Frank remained deep in thought, his face downcast. When he glanced at his watch, he pulled himself to his full height, shoulders back. A soldier's stance. Stepping out into the hallway, he reassumed his characteristic swagger and jovial demeanor.

Martha sat on a bench in the garden and watched as Frank approached along the flagstone pathway, a tiny curl of a smile playing on his lips when he saw her.

"Greetings, ma'am, you are still looking lovely," he said as he made a sweeping bow, hat in hand. "It's been a long time."

"Yes, it has, Frank. Decades, in fact. Nice to see you again."

"Nice to see you, too. I wanted to talk with you earlier today, but we didn't have a chance." He paused and twisted his hat nervously in his hands. "I was surprised to see your name among the guests for this tour. Of course, I couldn't be sure it was you," continued Frank. "There must be other Martha Stantons in the world." He paused. "Before we parted company in 'Nam, I probably should have told you about Nancy, back home. But we lived minute-by-minute back then, didn't we?"

"That we did," agreed Martha. "Those were the rules. No expectations."

"Just curious, Martha, did you know it was my tour company?"

"No. How would I have known? Just a strange coincidence, I guess." Martha looked at Frank and shook her head, irritation creasing her brow.

An uncomfortable pause in the conversation caused them both to stare at the fading light playing across the lawn.

"Lovely garden, isn't it?" said Frank, in an attempt to relieve the awkward silence. "Best we've seen on our tour today. Especially those roses." His voice became wistful. "My wife's favorite flower."

"Are they?" Martha glanced over at the fragrant peony hedge beyond the rose garden. "They do smell nice, but I'm not fond of the thorns. I prefer peonies."

"Nancy always said that the thorns made them all the sweeter. She said it was worth the risk of getting scratched for the reward of the lovely flower and the magnificent scent."

"And how is Nancy these days, Frank?"

Frank sighed. "Nancy died. Cancer. Two years ago, almost. Can't believe it's been that long already."

"Oh. Sorry, Frank. I didn't know." Martha pulled a leaf from a rose bush, twirled it in her fingers absently and dropped it. "I'm sure that must be very difficult for you."

"Some days are worse than others, but it's getting better," he said. "It's just when I see things she loved— like these roses—it makes me miss her more. And I'll admit I deeply regret not spending more time with her before she got sick, but I was on the road so much with my jobs…"

"Of course, we all want to justify our regrets, don't we?"

Frank gave her a pained look.

"Now, if I may change the subject once again, that's a glorious sunset, isn't it?" She pointed to the sky.

"Indeed, it is. Outstanding," said Frank.

They spent the next few moments in silent appreciation. Pink, purple and dark blue clouds painted the sky as a neon-orange sun began to drop behind the mountains.

"Frank, do you ever think of those days in 'Nam?" asked Martha. "Those crazy, perilous times we had? Honestly, I'm surprised you've become a garden tour guide after all of the bizarre risks you took back then."

"I was much younger," said Frank. "And if I remember correctly, you didn't exactly stay home and knit either."

"True. It was an exciting time to be a journalist. Especially for a greenhorn like me. It was such a thrill when I got the assignment to cover the Marine Corps. It scared me out of my wits, but it was a huge honor to be trusted with so much crucial information."

"We sure had some good times back then, though, didn't we? Remember the chaos of '73?" asked Frank. "Through it all, you still managed to get your stories written and out to the press on time. Amazing."

Martha traced her finger around a chubby cherub on the arm of the garden bench. "And as dangerous and horrible as it was, 'Nam gave my writing career the kickstart it needed." She sighed. "I've devoted my life to chasing stories, although now they're much tamer stories."

"No family? You didn't marry? Somehow, I had the impression you'd settle down one day. You know, leave all of the risky reporting behind you."

"No. No white picket fence for me. I kept chasing that story that would change the world."

"And look where it led you," said Frank. "Right here on a garden tour in little Custer's Mill with an old pal from days gone by. Life throws us some curveballs once in a while, doesn't it?"

"Sure does," said Martha. "But enough about ancient times. So what are you doing leading a garden tour? As the owner of the company, I'd think you'd have tour guides to do that for you."

"Perhaps I should ask what you're doing on a garden tour?" said Frank, smiling.

"That's easy. I'm writing a story for a Virginia gardening magazine."

"My reason is a little less direct than yours. I sometimes take the tours myself to be sure they're up to my satisfaction," he said smugly.

"On this particular tour, I'm killing two birds with one stone and accompanying two young folks who recently joined my other company, Living Healthy."

"My, my, garden tours and Living Healthy. You certainly have a lot of irons in the fire, don't you, Frank?" said Martha with more than a hint of sarcasm.

"I've several business ventures actually." Frank shrugged. "You know what they say, 'jack-of-all-trades, master-of-none.'"

"Hmm… I see," remarked Martha. "As I remember, you managed to always come away from any venture unscathed."

"Not quite sure where you are going with that, but the young couple Andy and Sarah, just recently signed on to sell products for Living Healthy, my latest venture. This tour is a sign-on bonus, and I decided to come along to get to know them a little better. It helps that I own both businesses."

"Not to put too fine a point on it, but they don't seem interested in getting to know you or anyone else. What does your company sell?"

Frank slipped into sales mode. "We offer meals that are healthy, low-fat, and enhanced with our patented, high-energy vitamin mix."

"Hmm. Okay," said Martha in a disinterested voice.

"You should give it a try, Martha. You can get a three-month subscription to sample it. Or you can also get a six-month or a twelve-month subscription to make sure you have healthy food choices all year long."

"No thanks, Frank. Sounds too much like a tier marketing scheme to me. One of those network sales things."

"We're legit, Martha. You don't think I'd try to cheat people, do you?" Frank looked offended.

If Martha paused a second longer than necessary before she answered, Frank didn't seem to notice. "No, of course not. Sorry, Frank."

Frank nodded. "Apology accepted."

Martha stood up. "Well, I'm exhausted. Think I'll turn in for the night." She raised her hand to her forehead in a salute. "Later then. Sir."

"At ease, civilian," said Frank.

She walked back toward the house, leaving Frank standing in the garden. He scratched his chin and shrugged, then seated himself on the bench vacated by Martha.

In his customary fashion, he addressed his dead wife. "Well, Nancy, that was the reporter I told you about. Martha Stanton. And like I always said, I never made her any promises in 'Nam. My heart was always yours, Nan. Always yours. "He fell into a silent reverie.

After several minutes he roused himself and trudged back toward the mansion and the lights twinkling in its windows.

***

Glenda and Isobel Fischer were sisters, but one would never guess their relationship by appearance alone. Glenda was short, pudgy, and soft. Her fluffy white hair curled around her plump face, framing it in snow white tendrils. Her voice was cheery with only a slight trace of her native German accent.

Isobel, on the other hand, was tall, angular, and thin. Her straight, short, iron-grey hair gave her a stern appearance, and she had not learned to soften the hard sounds of her first language.

The sisters sat in on the burgundy settee in the large parlor, sipping iced tea from delicate crystal glasses.

"I don't know if I can take another steamy day like this one." Glenda dabbed at her cheeks with a small, embroidered handkerchief. "I hope Monticello is cooler than the state arboretum. It was lovely but so hot."

Isobel nodded. "I don't know how you convinced me to take this garden tour. I'd rather be back at home sitting in the air-conditioned library working on our family research."

"Oh Izzy, you take life too seriously. Our musty ancestors will still be in their crumbling books long after the tour is over. You have the entire winter to untangle the branches of our family tree. Besides, she added, her voice lowering, "there are ever so many nice things here. Antiques, if I'm not mistaken. And expensive crystal." She held her glass up to inspect it.

Isobel nodded. "You have a point there, sister. You have a definite point."

The women looked at the silver spoons on the tea tray. "Antique Victorian, if I'm not mistaken," said Glenda as she slipped two spoons into the large pocket of her sundress.

***

Sarah sat in front of the bay window in the bedroom. Her husband reclined on the plush pillows adorning the antique four-poster bed. His arms were tucked behind his head. A folder lay open with spreadsheets and colorful pamphlets splayed across a small table by the window, and the last rays of sun filtered through the white lace curtains leaving long patterns of roses across the table. "I read that roses could mean either a blessing or a curse," she said."I wonder if it's a sign—probably a curse, knowing our luck." She propped her head on her hands and sighed as her shoulders slumped.

"Frank Wright was so convincing," said Andy. "Who would've thought that he'd misrepresent the truth to such an extent? 'Buy in,' he said. 'You're young. You'll be millionaires before you're forty.' Well, look at us now. Twenty-eight and broke. And Frank acts like this so-called bonus garden tour is his great gift to us. As if it would make up for the money we've lost."

"Okay, Andy, let's assume you're right, this is a scam," Sarah spoke in an urgent tone. "Our savings are gone, all $10,000! But what can we do about it now?"

"I don't know. It's not my fault." Andy's voice rose. "But we can't sit and take it. I know I can't sit and take it. Not only did we get swindled by this man, but I got my mom involved too."

He jumped up suddenly and began to pace back and forth across the room. "Mom trusted me and she has such a small retirement income. She can't keep making these payments. How could I have been so stupid to get her involved?" He sank back onto the bed.

Sarah's eyes softened. "You weren't stupid, only trusting. "She went to stand beside him and took his hand. "Sorry if it sounded like I was blaming you. I'm not. We trusted the information Frank gave us. We thought we'd be able to make enough to buy a house in just a year. But he failed to tell us all the hidden costs that would be passed on to our customers."

"Yeah, how do we continue selling these meal packages in good conscience, and how do we get our money back out?" Andy said. "We don't, and we don't. "He balled his hands into fists and pounded his thighs for emphasis.

"Maybe Frank didn't know either. He did tell us it was a new venture for him also, and he used his savings too. Maybe he got scammed like we did," said Sarah.

"There you go, Sarah, your little Pollyanna attitude comes to the rescue once again."

"I'm simply trying to help, Andy." Sarah's lip started to quiver. "This is a bad situation. My father warned you to do some investigating before you put all of our savings into this man's hands. You know what he always says. 'If it's too good to be true…'"

"I know, I know. With you it's always, 'Daddy said this, Daddy said that.' I'm sick of hearing how the amazing Colonel Westmoreland is always right. Meaning I'm always wrong. And I'm sick of Frank Wright and how he's screwed up my life." He paused. "Our life."

Andy's phone rang, breaking the silence that hung in the air.

“Mom, hi! Yes, we made it just fine,” said Andy. “Don’t worry about us.” Andy looked at Sarah and shrugged. “What? Oh, the B&B is nice. Sarah says it’s quaint and charming. No, I haven’t had a chance to talk with Frank.”

Andy began to pace as he spoke, struggling to maintain false cheerfulness in his tone. “I will though, soon,” he said. “I don’t want you to worry about anything. Okay. Love you, too, Mom. Bye.” Andy dropped his phone on the bed. His shoulders sagged.

“I sure hope we can work all this out somehow,” said Sarah.

Andy punched his hands into the pillows. “We will. We will work it out. I don’t know how, but one way or another, I’m gonna make this right, Sarah. I’m gonna make this right.”

Tuesday Morning

May 28

The early morning sky was still dark as Jake drove Emma and Kate along the rutted lane to Nanette's farm. Jake hoped his car's suspension was up to the task.

"Daddy, Nanette says we might get to see some baby goats get born today!"

"That so, Kit Kat?" said Jake. He glanced over his shoulder as he drove.

Kate bounced up and down with excitement, despite her seatbelt. For once her long strawberry blonde hair didn't flop down into her eyes. Emma knew Jake's hairdressing abilities were less than stellar, so she'd offered to pull Kate's unruly mop into a neat ponytail before they left her townhouse.

Nanette stood at the door of the white farmhouse and gestured them inside. "Come on in, folks!" she said. "Beautiful morning shaping up."

The farm kitchen was a scene right out of the 1950s. The pale yellow enameled cabinets topped with sage green counters, stood on faded linoleum floors. Floral-patterned curtains fluttered in the fresh morning breeze.

"Guess what, Kate? Four new kids were born two days ago, and I still have one momma goat ready to deliver any time. We'll just have to wait and see if she gives birth today." She paused. "In any case, the newborns will keep you entertained, young lady. You'd think they have springs for legs, the way they bounce around. Sort of like you this morning. Bubbly and full of spirit."

Jake inhaled the aroma of meat browning on the stove. "Mmm. Smells like stew is on your menu today." His voice held a tinge of envy. "We're taking breakfast up to the mountains with us, coffee and bagels."

"All right." Nanette folded her arms and shook her head. "I'll send a few helpings of stew home with you both when you come back. You and Emma will need a hearty lunch after your hike." She nodded toward Emma.

"Thanks, Nanette, that sounds great," said Emma. "We'll stop by and pick up some bread to go with your stew at Glen's Market on our way back...enough for all of us." She stood up, ready to be off. This day would be a long one. First, the mysterious discussion during the hike, then a full day of work at the library. And so much catching up to do after her vacation.

"Make sure it's that good, crispy kind, nothing mushy. Can't abide mushy bread," said Nanette.

"Will do," agreed Emma. "And now Jake and I had better be off or we'll miss our chance to get to the top of Mary's Rock without a big crowd already there. It's best there in the early morning."

They headed out to Jake's truck and drove down the long lane, waving to Nanette and Kate until they were out of sight.

The morning was clear and cool, perfect hiking weather. Later in the day the temperature would approach 80. But a morning mist still hovered in the hollows as they crossed over New Market Gap. Green rolling pastures dotted with cattle stretched across Page Valley to the Blue Ridge Mountains on the far side of the valley. Fields of hay stood ripening and almost ready for an early harvest. They rode in silence, both content to enjoy the wide-open views.

The road narrowed and became steep and curvy as they headed up into the Blue Ridge.

"Oh, look!" Emma exclaimed and pointed at six deer grazing inside the forest beside the curving highway. "Such beautiful creatures. I'd love to see some on our hike."

"Me too. Might see some at this early hour," said Jake, pulling into the entrance to Skyline Drive. "Almost there." He stopped at the gate and pulled out his pass.

Emma saw with satisfaction that only two other cars were in the parking lot. It would be much more crowded when they returned. She grabbed her backpack and handed Jake his. Her stomach was already growling, but they'd planned to eat breakfast at the top.

A beautiful view from the trail was almost constant. The mountainside dropped away steeply as they wound their way upward. A runner passed them with a light tread on the rocky path of sharp shale and rounded the curve ahead. "How in the world does he do that without slipping on this trail?" asked Emma.

"Practice, Emma. Practice. You could do it, too, if you worked up to it."

"I think I'll keep my running limited to the flatlands." Emma laughed, and as she turned to look at Jake, she tripped on a large rock. Jake grabbed her hand to steady her and continued to hold it after she'd regained her balance. They walked along in silence, the only sound the crunching of their boots on the path.

Emma wondered if she should leave her hand in Jake's or pull away. What was he thinking? Her heart pounded as much from Jake's nearness as from the incline of the trail.

"You know, Emma, I really missed you when you took your trip to Europe. Before you left, you said something about maybe taking a job somewhere else. I sure hope not. A guy like me knows a lot of people, but we don't have real friends. I consider you a real friend."

Emma gently disengaged her hand and made a pretense of bending down to re-tie her boot.

"And I consider you a real friend, too, Jake. Both you and Kate."

"Kate is causing me some concern these days."

"Why? Is she getting in trouble at school or something?" Emma was alarmed.

"Oh no. Nothing like that," said Jake. "It's just that I have an appointment with my attorney, Paul Stewart, later this morning. I really need to name a guardian for Kate. You know, in case something happens to me. When I had that truck accident up on North Mountain last year, it occurred to me that if I die, Billy Brubaker could be named as Kate's next-of-kin. I can't let that happen."

"Wait. What? You've gotta be kidding! No, you certainly can't let that happen," responded Emma. "So what are you going to do?"

"Well, I know this is asking a lot, and it's kind of soon after your trip...but I was wondering if...wondering if...." Jake paused and stopped walking to look at Emma. He cleared his throat.

Emma felt a moment of panic. Oh no, she thought, he's not going to propose, is he? Not now. Not when I'm starting to get myself together. With effort, she maintained her poise. Should she stop him?

Before she could speak, Jake took her hand in his. "Emma. This is hard for me, but I want to know if you would consider being Kate's guardian. If I die." He released her hand and stared at the ground. "I know it's a huge thing to ask, but Kate loves you and you'd make a great mo… role model for her."

Emma stared at Jake's bent head. Not a proposal then. A legal arrangement. Well, she had to smile at herself for jumping to conclusions. But he did hold her hand…

"Jake, I don't think this is a good time in my life to take on such a responsibility," said Emma. "In fact, I'm not completely certain I'll stay in Custer's Mill. I learned a lot about myself when I traveled to Europe, and there are some areas where I plan to make significant improvements. Like self-confidence and not being such a touchy and needy person. I want to be the kind of person who can stand up for what's right, but not get my feelings hurt when everyone doesn't love me for it."

"Well, I think you're great the way you are, Emma," said Jake. They resumed walking, now passing a sign for the Appalachian Trail. Jake didn't return to his request.

"And here we are. Mary's Rock."

They stepped around the final curve on the trail. It opened out into a circle of huge boulders with almost 360-degree views of the valleys below. Two other hikers lounged in the sun and nodded to acknowledge the newcomers.

Jake and Emma climbed up onto a flat spot and spread out their breakfast. Coffee, bagels, cream cheese and strawberry jam. The morning mist had burned off, and tiny farms, fields, and roadways appeared far below. The air was already starting to warm, although cool currents still swept up through the cracks in the rocks.

"Jake, you know who would make a wonderful guardian for Kate?" Emma's face was animated. "My great Uncle Albert. After all, he's Kate's great-grandfather. What could be more appropriate?"

"But he's old, Emma. What do I do if he dies?" asked Jake.

Emma spread a bagel with a thick layer of cream cheese and a dollop of jam. She took a big bite, and her response was muffled as she chewed. "How about you put Nanette as a second choice? If she's willing, that is. She's great with Kate. And let me think it over. I might agree to be one of your choices; just not the first choice. Or the second. Maybe the third."

Emma washed her food down with a swig of steaming coffee. "And, anyway, I hope you'll be around until Kate is an old woman herself. You might live to be a great-grandpa, you know." She took another big bite of bagel.

Jake looked thoughtful. Albert, Nanette and Emma. A good lineup for his sweet daughter. And he agreed with Emma. He hoped he'd be around a long time yet, long enough to be a great-grandfather. What a thought.

"Thanks, Emma," said Jake. "That's great advice. I'll ask Albert and Nanette as soon as I can. With you as the third choice, I could set my mind at ease."

They turned their attention to watching the activity in the farms below as they chewed and sipped in companionable silence.

When six more hikers appeared at the top of the trail, talking and laughing together, Emma glanced at her watch and then at Jake. He nodded. Time to head back down to the car. Jake extended a hand and pulled Emma to her feet.

"Thanks, Emma. You're the best."

"You're not too bad yourself, Jake." Emma laughed, jumping down off the boulder and on to the trail, happy to be on top of the world on a beautiful day. Happy to be in Jake's company.

***

The library would open in exactly seven minutes, and Emma had at least another hour's worth of mail to sort. She stuck a pencil behind one ear, dislodging a brown curl from its clip. After the glow of her morning hike, she was already feeling the stress of too much to do. Several patrons milled around the door. Once in a while Emma opened up a few minutes early. But not today.

Thank heaven her assistant, Cara, would be here soon. Until this past spring, Emma had been the only paid staff member at the library. When she announced her plans to travel to Europe, the town council had finally agreed to fork over the money for an assistant. As far as she could tell, Cara had done an excellent job of taking care of the library for the two weeks Emma was away.

Emma was glad that the council members trusted her with the hiring process. She knew exactly the kind of person she was looking for. After interviewing several applicants, she found a perfect match. Cara Donovan, a recent graduate of the University of Kentucky, had a brand-new library science degree, and she was excited to put her knowledge to practical use. She was friendly, patient, and helpful. Already she had taken over story hour and was eagerly planning a teen book club for the summer.

But Emma still missed the down-to-earth, sensible work of her three regular volunteers—her library ladies. She hoped they would be back on the schedule soon. Of course, she was happy for Nanette, Jane, and Marguerite and their successful venture with tearoom and the B&B. And she realized that the ladies had their hands full with planning, decorating, and booking guests. But things weren't the same without them.

Even though she was swamped, she wouldn't have traded her European vacation for all of the clutter-free desks in the world. England, Germany, France, Switzerland, and Belgium. One of those 'five countries in fourteen days' tours. Places she and Eric had planned to travel to when they finished college.

Eric had been her first real boyfriend. And there had been a time when she thought he would be her only true love. How naive she had been in those days. But perhaps she was too hard on herself. Eric could have meant what he said. He really might have wanted to travel the world with her. But she'd never know. Eric was dead, killed in a fire at a college party caused by carelessness and too many candles. Serafina had invited him to the party and he had gone. Like a sheep to the slaughter. Like most men around Serafina.

But her trip had given Emma a new perspective. There was no reason she had to plant herself in Custer's Mill. She could still pursue some of the dreams she thought she had forgotten about.

An image of Jake Preston flashed across her mind. Could she leave Jake back in Custer's Mill while she explored the world? Before her trip, she would have said no, but now she wasn't sure. She thought maybe she and Jake could have a future together. But Jake was still grieving the death of his young wife, Mirabelle. It might take him years to move on. And then where would she be? A spinster librarian with a pile of books and a boatload of unfulfilled dreams.

She jumped as a harsh buzz sounded from the back door. Her forearm caught a stack of envelopes and journals and sent them scattering across the floor. She bent down to pick them up, bumping her head on the desk as she straightened back up.

Great, she thought. If this is how my day is shaping up, maybe I'd better go back to Mary's Rock. Installing the buzzer and keypad was a good idea, but she wondered if she'd ever get used to the rasping sound. It still startled her every time it rang.

"Yoo-hoo! Anybody home?"

The familiar voice sent a wave of irritation over Emma. She didn't want to deal with Serafina now. When they were children, Serafina, Emma and Sissy, Hiram's daughter, had been inseparable. Serafina was their ring-leader, ever the risk-taker—exhilarating but irritating, free-spirited but troublesome and dangerous. Wasn't Serafina partially responsible for

Eric's death? At least Emma thought so.

But how long could one live in the past? It was obvious that Serafina felt none of the guilt that Emma silently heaped on her. Perhaps she should try to repair the damaged relationship with her former best friend. Emma took a deep breath and turned to Serafina.

"Serafina. Lovely to see you. How did you get in? New keypad hack?"

"I wish." Serafina said. She floated by Emma trailing the scent of patchouli, like a lovely wood nymph with her ginger locks loose and flowing behind her.

Emma, however, was not impressed.

"Not as sophisticated as that," said Serafina. "Cara gave me the code while you were away."

"Oh really?" Emma struggled to hide her annoyance. She would have to have a heart-to-heart with Miss Cara.

"Oh, don't be such a grump. I told her that you threatened to call the police if I picked the lock again. And I also told her that I was your best friend and that you'd be fine with me having the code."

"I guess it would be too much to ask that you wait a minute and a half until the library actually opens?"

"Probably." Serafina grinned. "Come on, I just need to make a copy of this price list before I open my shop this morning. This company is always changing the prices. I can never keep up with them. When I try to balance my sales against the inventory costs, it never seems to come out right."

Emma bit her tongue. Serafina never took notice of details. In math class she always rounded numbers and estimated. It wasn't that Emma was obsessive about small things, but sometimes details mattered--like when you balanced checkbooks or resolved inventory costs. She took the paper form from Serafina. "Just one copy?"

"Seriously? No ranting? No raving?" Serafina raised an eyebrow. "You must still be asleep."

Emma moved toward the copy machine. Raising the cover, she placed the document on the glass. She was not going to let Serafina get under her skin. "You got this, girl," she whispered to herself.

***

"Black tea again, Isobel?" Glenda scowled as her sister poured a thick stream of dark liquid into a delicate china cup. "Why don't we have our tea in the parlor with the others? They have lovely muffins and other goodies down there, no doubt. Why must you make this inky tar in our rooms? That electric teapot hardly heats the water."

"I can't imagine it would matter what kind of tea you drink, Glenda. You fill the cup with so much milk and sugar. There's hardly any room left for tea."

"Well maybe, Isobel, if you would make some sweet, fruity tea, I wouldn't have to add other things to make it drinkable."

Isobel set the pot on a small side table and covered it with a quilted tea cozy. "Wilhelm used to make peppermint tea. Remember? He grew mint up by the springhouse."

"Of course, I remember, sister," said Glenda. "How could I ever forget anything our dear brother did?"

"Dear Wilhelm." Isobel took a sip of the hot liquid.

"Mother said he was an angel from heaven, and Papa worshiped the ground he walked on."

"They were grateful they finally had a son." Isobel pulled the silk curtains away from the bedroom window. A ray of light shone through the ancient bubble-glass panes. "Now, enough of this useless talk. Did you count the silver like I asked you to this morning?"

Glenda added another lump of sugar to her cup and scowled at Isobel. "I don't know why you make me count the silver coins every single day. What do you think is going to happen to them? They're locked in the strongbox."

"Glenda," said Isobel, her voice dangerously soft. "Did you or did you not count the silver?"

"Yes, I counted the silver," said Glenda. "The 1881 Morgan silver dollar. All seven of the Peace Silver Dollars, and all of the Eisenhowers."

Isobel nodded. "Good. We must never let our most valuable pieces slip through our fingers."

"But I don't see why we should have to carry them everywhere we go." Glenda pushed the heavy metal box under the bed. "It's annoying."

"You think our wealth is annoying?" said Isobel.

"But they're not worth that much," said Glenda wearily. "The appraiser said we'd get no more than $3,500 for the entire bunch."

Isobel shook her head. "There's more to that collection than meets the eye."

Glenda rolled her eyes. "Some people say there's more to you than meets the eye."

Isobel set her teacup on a flowered coaster next to the bed and glared at her sister. "We leave for Monticello in 15 minutes. I'll go down to the parlor and wait for you there," she said. "Since I don't appear to be welcome here."

***

"Brubaker, eh? Any relation to the folks who own the Brubaker mansion?" Frank leaned up in his seat so his mouth was near Billy Brubaker's ear. "That's pretty funny. Bus driver Brubaker driving us from the former Brubaker mansion."

Billy's clenched his jaw and his hands tightened on the steering wheel as he merged on to the interstate. "Nothing funny about it. Miss Bertha Brubaker was my aunt."

Just two weeks ago, Billy had purchased the 12-passenger van to start a new chapter in his life—offering transport services to travel groups like the garden club. He told folks he hoped to branch out into a shuttle service up to Dulles International Airport, since Greyhound no longer served the region. A magnetic sign proclaiming "Brubaker Transport" decorated the side of the spotless white exterior.

Frank continued to hold a one sided conversation with Billy until he gave up and sat back in his seat. The passengers talked quietly, enjoying the passing views of rolling fields and farms that reached to the foot of the Blue Ridge Mountains.

As they crossed the pass on Afton Mountain, Billy pulled over to let the group take photos at the panoramic overlook.

Billy was rubbing at a smear of dirt on the side of the van when Andy came up beside him and said in a loud whisper, "Just so you know, man, none of us can stand Frank Wright and his big mouth. Sorry you have to be nice to him."

Billy nodded and shrugged. "Thanks. Well, it's time we get moving so we can get to Monticello before it's too crowded."

As soon as the van pulled back onto the interstate, Frank leaned up in his seat and spoke over Billy's shoulder. "Think this buggy will make it down the mountain?". I've heard it can be pretty rough in the fog."

"Considering the fact that it's sunny and dry, I don't see fog as a problem. I have confidence in my vehicle." Billy changed to a lower gear and the van jerked slightly.

"Want me to teach you how to drive a stick shift?" Frank chuckled.

Billy gritted his teeth. "I'm just a little bit out of practice. I haven't been driving this thing too long."

"That's comforting," Frank said, letting out a sigh that said otherwise. "How many miles to Monticello?"

"GPS says 25.3. Should get there in about 25 minutes."

"Well, that's a relief. You going to take the tour too?"

"Nah, I brought a book. Planning to sit in the van and read until you all are ready to head to the vineyards. I've seen Monticello plenty of times."

The rest of the trip was quiet. Frank had either dozed off or found other ways to occupy his time. Billy concentrated on maneuvering the van through the late morning traffic.

He pulled the bus into the visitor's parking lot and opened the doors for his passengers. Frank rushed ahead of the others to get in line. Martha smiled absently at Billy, and Andy gave him a knowing look.

The two elderly sisters were the last to climb out of the van.

"Ladies?" Billy offered his hand to help them make the final step down to the gravel parking lot, but only Glenda allowed him to assist her.

With any luck, the Monticello shuttle bus would arrive soon.

***

"I loved Jefferson's house, but now we're moving along too fast to enjoy the grounds," grumbled Martha. She picked up her pace to keep up with the rest of the group. Every time she'd stopped to take photos, the group would move ahead without her.

"Oh, I think that English lavender is worth the whole trip," said Glenda as she crushed a fragrant, purple bud in her hand. "The scent is glorious! And that vegetable garden—amazing."

"True," agreed Martha. I plan to write an entire article devoted to Mr. Jefferson's green thumb. But I had hoped to see some Joseph's Coat or Love-Lies-Bleeding in the wooded areas."

"What an awful name for a flower." Glenda shuddered. "Love-Lies-Bleeding!"

"It does look like big globs of blood dripping from the plant stalk." Frank joined the group, seeming to delight in Glenda's squeamishness.

"It's actually a delicacy in some parts of the world," said Martha. "It's good for you."

"Seriously?" said Frank. "People eat that stuff?"

"Yes. In Indonesia they sauté it with chilies and spices," said Martha. "And in some countries, they eat the raw leaves like spinach."

"Give me a rare steak any day," said Frank shaking his head at the folly of eating plant leaves. "Speaking of rare steaks, is it lunchtime yet?"

"The B&B ladies gave Mr. Brubaker a lunch basket for us, but we need to finish this tour first so we can take the shuttle back to the parking lot," said Glenda. "I'd be happy to go back right now and ask him to find us a picnic table. It's such a lovely day for a picnic. My feet hurt anyway, and I'd like to sit down."

"That would be very kind, madam," said Frank with a flourish of his hand. "Tell Brubaker we'll be back by 1:00 and hungry as bears."

***

Billy had the picnic set up when the rest of group returned. He retreated to a table nearby, in an attempt to avoid the boorish Frank Wright and his condescending comments over lunch. To no avail.

"Bill! Bill, come over here and join us." Frank Wright turned around on the picnic bench and motioned to Billy. "Unlike Mr. Jefferson, we'll let the help share our table. Modern times, you know?"

Billy sighed and trudged over to their table.

"Would you care for some iced tea?" asked Glenda, holding out a plastic cup.

"Yes, thank you, ma'am," said Billy. He sat on the edge of the picnic bench, keeping as much distance as possible from the group.

The group tucked into the roast beef and turkey sandwiches with gusto, and ate in relative silence. They spoke only when they wanted the bag of chips or plate of relishes to be passed around. It was warm, and Glenda kept their cups filled with sweet tea.

After five minutes of blessed peace and quiet, Frank Wright picked up the thread of his earlier conversation. "So, what's it feel like, Brubaker, being the hired hand serving the people who are staying at your family mansion? Must rankle."

"I'm happy to be working at my own business, sir," Billy said.

"Hmmm," said Frank. "I'd think it would rankle. Know it would if I were in your shoes."

"I guess it's a good thing you're in your own shoes then, isn't it?" said Billy, standing abruptly.

Billy addressed the group. "You all take your time, and just let me know when you're ready to head back. I'll pack up the lunch things."

After everyone had eaten their fill, they all sauntered off among the trees as Billy repacked the van, his thoughts dark and troubled. "That boor, Frank Wright," he muttered under his breath. "I should keep away from him or I'll do something I'll regret." He paused and stared at Frank chatting with the other guests under a huge white oak tree. "But it's true. I never thought I'd be serving lunch and carting around such a self-absorbed bunch of people." He closed the hatch of the van with a vicious shove. "Guess Dad was right after all. He always said I'd amount to nothing."

Tuesday Afternoon

May 28

Serafina unlocked the door of the Serendipity Herb & Tea Shop and walked to the back of the large room in the old warehouse. Several boxes were stacked against the open wall studs. Her cat blinked at her from his perch on the top box.

"Well, Midnight, even though that prissy Emma Kramer gave me a hard time earlier about faxing this order, I got what I needed. She waved a paper in the air. "Emma is so predictable. Eric may have liked her, but he said he said I was full of fire and life." She stroked the cat's sleek black fur.

A forlorn expression crossed her face. "I don't feel very lively anymore, though. In fact, I think the fire's gone out." She stared into the distance for a few moments, then shook her head. "But…there's work to be done. And you have to move, my feline friend," she said. "It's time to get this shipment unloaded and bagged up. Nobody's going to buy it while it's sitting here in boxes." The cat made an irritated chirp as she lifted him down onto the floor. He stalked off behind the shelving, tail held high.

Working without a break, Serafina unpacked her tea and herbs and piled them on the counter. She made precise inventory notes in her ledger as she worked. She had to keep better track of expenses if she wanted her shop to survive. By three o'clock, only a single box remained. Using the box cutter, she sliced the tape and pulled the box open. But this box was not part of the tea shipment. She sat back on her heels, momentarily puzzled.

The box held items she had never unpacked after she returned from Europe. Colorful skirts. A thick sweater. Dancing shoes. A glossy flyer in English was tucked along one side of the box, and she pulled it out, her heart pounding. The front of the brochure showed a photo of Serafina in her bright Roma outfit, twirling around a man who held her hand. *Roma Dancers to Perform in Munich*, the headline announced.

Feelings long suppressed surged through her. Bits of dance music came to her mind unbidden. She was desperate to instruct her racing thoughts. Not now. Not here. It's over. She slid the flyer back into the box and hastily closed the lid.

Pandora's Box. That's what it was. She shoved the box as far back in the corner as she could and shuddered.

***

Stewart, Stewart, & Sampson, Attorneys at Law, had been the only law practice in Custer's Mill for decades. The old Victorian on Main Street that housed the family business was an institution in the community. The firm had been passed down through successive generation. Paul Stewart V knew there was never any question of his vocation. He was a Stewart, and he would be a lawyer. He had apprenticed under his father, Paul Stewart IV. Upon graduation from the University of Virginia, Paul joined his father and aunt, Pauline Stewart Sampson, in the family business. Paul was the sixth and last generation of Stewarts. He had never married, so the Stewart line stopped with him. The legal offices had always been on the main floor while living quarters were upstairs. He had never known another home or place of business.

A slender man in his early fifties, Paul held his six-foot frame ramrod straight. The graying hair at his temples added to his distinguished looks. He was rarely seen in anything other than a three-piece suit. Pulling down the cuff of his shirt, as if it wasn't the perfect one-inch length beyond the edge of his jacket sleeve, he leaned over to reach his phone and push the button to speak to his receptionist. "Linda, please send in Mr. Preston. Thank you."

As the large, carved door opened, he came around his desk to greet the young man. The same desk his father and grandfather had used before him.

He gave Jake a warm handshake. "Jake, good to see you. It's been a while. Everything going well with Kate's endowment? Checks arriving regularly, I presume." Paul settled into his swivel chair and motioned for Jake to take one of the blue leather seats in front of the desk

"No problems there, Paul. I do worry that Kate's expenses each month don't require such a large sum of money," said Jake. "I end up putting the rest in her college account." Jake frowned. "Should I have come to you about that—the checks are for more money than Kate needs?"

"No, no." The lawyer laughed. "We rarely hear that we give someone too much money. It's a modest sum compared to her inheritance, I assure you. And the rest of her funds are growing nicely. We keep track of those things for you, of course. The benefit of a small-town law firm is that we give our clients personal attention." Paul smiled. "Now, how can I help you?"

"Well, to be honest, it's taken me a while for the magnitude of Kate's inheritance to sink in and realize my responsibilities as her trustee." Jake took a deep breath. "I have to tell you—at times it scares me." Jake pulled a sheaf of papers out of the folder he carried into the room.

"It is a goodly sum," agreed Paul.

"So much money." Jake shook his head. "Last year, when I sat in your conference room with Billy, Sissy, and the library ladies, I had no idea our lives would be impacted like this by Miss Bertha's will. I was shocked when you told us the papers Miss Bertha found proved my late wife, Mirabelle, was related to the Brubaker family. But it's still hard to imagine that my Kate and Billy are related."

"Yes, and I remember how upset Billy Brubaker was, but that has all seemed to sort itself out. The ladies received the mansion and have made quite a nice bed & breakfast of the old place. Billy did have debts and fines to pay, but he still managed to keep some of his inheritance." The lawyer looked over his glasses with concern. "Billy isn't making any trouble for you and Kate?"

"No, nothing like that, it's just…you know the line of work I'm in. Being a police chief in Custer's Mill is better than a county detective, but there is still the element of risk each day. Last fall, I had an incident on the mountain that gave me concern for Kate if something should happen to me. After Mirabelle's death, I've taken care of our daughter all by myself. It hasn't been easy, but I wouldn't change anything—except having Mirabelle with us."

"Yes, I can imagine the pressure your job adds to being a single parent," said Paul. "Do you mind telling me about Mirabelle and how she died?"

"It was a car accident," said Jake. "She was really excited about going to this concert. She loved being a violinist in the community orchestra in Winchester. It had been a long day, and I backed out of going with her at the last minute. I should have been there. She shouldn't have gone alone..." Jake's voice trailed off.

"You can't blame yourself. We all have regrets, things we wish we had done, but no amount of wishing can change fate. You're a good man, Jake Preston, and your wife would be proud of how well you have taken care of your daughter."

"I hope that would be the case." Jake shifted in his chair. "Every time I look at Kate, I see Mirabelle. She has her mother's strawberry blonde hair and bright blue eyes. She's headstrong and has a mind of her own. It worries me sometimes how independent Kate is becoming."

"Well, I can understand the worry any single parent would have for the care of their child. Do you have a guardian appointed for Kate if something should happen?"

"No, I don't, and that's why I'm here," said Jake. "I realized that if I don't assign a guardian the courts might give Kate to Billy." Jake's voice held a note of panic. "Paul, that is unacceptable."

The lawyer leaned back in his chair as if this thought had propelled him backward. "Yes, I can see how this would be disturbing. I don't think Billy would bring any harm to the child, but he isn't the most responsible person, nor is he the most trustworthy. I wouldn't want to see Kate or her money under his direction."

Jake nodded. "Now, you see my dilemma."

"I do, and we can sort this out. We should draft a whole new will for you and include specific instructions for Kate should something happen. Of course, we don't expect this will ever be needed, but we can plan for it, just in case.

"Good," said Jake. "The sooner the better. Paul, it has been such a burden on my mind lately."

Paul Stewart clasped his hands and leaned toward Jake. "Now, who do you wish to name as Kate's guardian?"

"I'm still working on that, but I have one person lined up and two other people in mind to ask. I'm hoping to name three people, to make sure I've taken care of Kate. Can I get back to you this week, and then I'll come in to sign the new will?

"Certainly," said Paul. "Just give me a call when you have the names, and we'll take care of it asap. Then you can rest easy."

***

"Gosh, Emma, I'm really sorry. I totally thought it would be okay to give Serafina the code. I mean she said she was your best friend and you wouldn't mind." A look of distress creased Cara's round face.

"Wait. Cara. Think about this. When have you ever seen Serafina and me hanging out? Or even talking? She is not my best friend. At least, not anymore. We grew up together, but she messed up any chance at friendship a long time ago."

Cara lowered her head. "I'm really sorry. She had me convinced that you two were best buddies."

"I'm not surprised. She could charm the stripes off a zebra. You'd be wise to stay clear of Serafina Wimsey."

Emma opened a small booklet and scanned the directions. "I'm going to put in a new code. Here, help me figure this out. "Emma squinted at the small print. "Hold down this button while I press the other two. These directions were obviously written for a three-handed person."

Cara smiled, her mood lifting at her boss's attempt at light humor. Short, plump and jolly, Cara's looks and personality were antithetical to the willowy, pensive Emma Kramer. Their mutual passion for books gave them common ground, however, and they worked well together. Both women sighed with relief as they heard two clicks and saw the lights on the keypad blink. "Okay, let's try this again." Emma scribbled a four-number sequence on a scrap of paper and handed it to Cara. "Memorize this and destroy the evidence," she said, pleased by their success at resetting the lock. "And," she added, "don't give out the numbers to anybody. Got it? Anybody. I'll make sure our volunteers get the code."

Cara nodded and glanced at her watch. "It's 5:15. Shall I shelve this last cart of books before I leave?"

Emma looked around the empty library. "No, go on home. I'm afraid if we hang out any longer, folks will be banging on the door to get back in."

"This sure is a popular place," said Cara. "Have a great evening. I'll see you in the morning."

Emma locked the door behind the young assistant and wandered back into her office. Although she'd recovered somewhat from jet lag after her trip, it would take a few days to get back into her regular work routine. Her desk was piled with flyers, catalogs, conference information—stacks of stuff that would eventually end up in the recycle bin.

She looked out the window. The mountains seemed to loom closer today than usual. Their high peaks and dipping valleys reminded her of Germany and Switzerland. She could completely understand why European immigrants chose to settle in the Shenandoah Valley. The landscape must have reminded them of home.

Hard to believe that last week at this time she had stood at the top of the Eiffel Tower watching the Seine flow right through the heart of Paris. Her mind began to scroll through the highlights of her trip, replaying them like a movie. She leaned back in her chair, straining to remember the sound of Big Ben chiming the hour and imagining the icy wind tangling her hair as she stood at the top of Mount Rigi in the Swiss Alps.

The Alps! Such beauty, but there was no one with her to share her amazement. She'd had to keep her thoughts to herself, diminishing the joy. It was hard not to long for Eric at those moments.

Emma stared out the window, remembering Eric's lopsided smile and his fondness for chocolate dip ice cream cones. Though they'd had fights, she couldn't remember anything they'd fought about. Perhaps memories improve with age, like fine wine, she thought.

She stood up with sudden resolve. Eric was dead, the Alps were beautiful, and she was lucky to have visited them. Memories of the past were sweet, but she needed to get on with the present, like thinking about Jake Preston and how he'd held her hand on the hike to Mary's Rock.

And in the present moment, her stomach was growling. First things first. It was time to focus on supper tonight. Emma laughed out loud, amused at her tendency for intorspective drama. She grabbed her bag and headed out the door, her thoughts turning to the immediate problem of which toppings to get on one of Sergio's thin crust pizzas.

Tuesday Evening

May 28

Terri adjusted the collar of the blue silk blouse and smiled at her reflection in the old gilt mirror over her dressing table. Yes. The perfect shade. Her eyes sparkled like sapphires under subtly mascaraed lashes. She felt confident Laurence would be dazzled. Or at least impressed.

She hadn't said anything to Aunt Jane about going out this evening. No need to stir up a lot of questions from that quarter. And she was grateful for Marguerite's offer to finish up in the kitchen after dinner. By now, the guests were either settled in their own rooms or strolling around the grounds. Of course, she'd be back in time to lock up for the night.

She was still a little surprised at herself for calling Laurence this morning and suggesting they meet for a late dinner tonight. She toyed with the idea of offering to cover his meal, but sensed his old-school sensibilities would be affronted if she did. She'd pay for her own meal, certainly.

They had agreed to meet for dinner at the new German restaurant in Mill City. Terri hadn't had Schweinebraten since she'd left Northern Virginia. She hoped the mushroom sauce wasn't too salty. There was nothing worse than paying for a meal that didn't suit the taste buds just right.

Laurence was waiting at their reserved table. He was dressed in light gray slacks, a cotton maroon shirt, and a charcoal sports jacket. He rose when he saw her.

"Good evening, Terri," he said, pulling out her chair and giving her an approving look.

"Good evening," said Terri. "This place is lovely. It's always a little tricky making reservations at a place you've never been. You look nice, Mr. George."

"And you as well, Miss Allman." Laurence smiled. "I know you're going to find this difficult to believe, but I've never eaten at a German restaurant before. In fact, I haven't experimented with many ethnic foods. You might say I've led a rather boring culinary life."

"There isn't an abundance of restaurant choices around here." Terri looked around. "But I think this was a good find."

Terri scanned the menu and immediately found what she was looking for. Schweinebraten with sour cream and mushroom sauce.

"Mind if I order the same?" asked Laurence. "I wouldn't know where to start with this menu. All of these bratens and schnitzels."

They sipped ice water and chatted. Small talk, but Terri was okay with that. Her track record with men wasn't exactly stellar. She didn't want to mess this up.

"How are things at the B&B?" asked Laurence.

"Intense," said Terri, smiling. "The ladies are running around like busy beavers and the guests are a bit demanding."

"When I saw the place, it all looked perfect. I can't imagine what they're finding to gripe about."

"Oh, complaints like the water is too tepid; the shower pressure is too low. We're new at this, you know. We'll improve."

“Sounds pretty stressful. I hope the ladies are holding up okay.”

“They just want to please everybody,” said Terri. The server placed two heaping plates of steaming pork in front of them.

“I could get used to this,” said Laurence picking up his fork. “Smells heavenly.”

Dinner went better than Terri had imagined. Both she and Laurence seemed reluctant to call it an evening. They lingered long after dessert. Neither one had brought up the subject of Alex, and Terri was glad. The fact that she'd been infatuated with Laurence's late brother might have made conversation awkward.

It was warm and humid when they left the restaurant. Rain was in the forecast for the next several days. Terri was sure he would kiss her or at least make another date when he said goodbye. She could tell he enjoyed being with her.

As they walked to Terri's car, the air crackled with romance. Laurence opened the car door for her and wished her a pleasant night. That was it. No hug, no light touch. No ‘I'd like to see you again.’ Not even a peck on the cheek. Terri wondered if she'd misread him.

After Terri drove off, Laurence sat in his truck a long time before he turned on the engine wondering to himself if he'd just messed up a wonderful evening. Terri seemed to like him. But she was so young, and he was so self-conscious and insecure. Most of his life he'd gotten along with bluster and bravado. But he found he could talk to Terri without all the swagger. But he couldn't allow himself to hope she could ever be serious about him. It was Alex she had loved. Not the older brother. Wasn't that how it had been most of his life? The girls would befriend him just to get close to Alex. He couldn't risk showing his feelings. He couldn't bear rejection. Not at this stage of life.

He drove down the empty street as the rain began to fall.

Wednesday Morning

May 29

Frank Wright sat alone at the large table in the dining room. Thin ribbons of sunlight shone through the windows creating bright stripes of burgundy and gold on the wool carpet. His hair was tousled and his eyes looked tired and worn. The grey whiskers on his unshaven face enhanced his disheveled appearance. He glanced up at the sound of footsteps descending the stairway.

Martha appeared in wide doorway and stood a moment with her hands on her hips. "I see you've beaten me to the first cup of joe," she said.

"Make that the third cup. A good morning to you, Martha!" Frank stood up and leaned against his chair. "I can't seem to clear my head this morning." He retrieved a small scone from the buffet and returned to his seat.

"Remember that black tar they used to give us in the mess tent?" asked Martha. She filled a delicate china cup with coffee from the pump pot on the buffet, and sat down at the table next to Frank. "I don't know how they could even call it coffee."

"I usually try to forget those days as much as I can," Frank shook his head and ran his hand over his bristly face. "I still can't look a can of Spam in the face."

"Ah yes," Martha said. "Specially Processed Army Meat."

"So. Tell me more about yourself, Martha," said Frank. "What's your schtick in the journalistic world? You only do garden stories these days?"

Martha gave him a sarcastic look. "I see you haven't kept up with my byline since Vietnam. Of course, why would you?" A flush crept up her cheeks. She studied her coffee intently, then took several dainty sips before continuing. "You had your life with your wife."

"Yes. Nancy was a real trooper. She kept the house, kept our life going while I was on tour. I was one of the lucky ones," said Frank. "I made it home." He stared off into the distance, lost in his thoughts.

After an uncomfortable silence, Martha busied herself topping off her coffee cup. Her hands shook, rattling the cup on the saucer and splattering drops of coffee onto the buffet. She dabbed a napkin at the spill. "Actually, Frank, I've reported on everything from homelessness to gardens, and my work has been published in major magazines and newspapers during my career," she said. "But no assignment ever lived up to the excitement of following your gang around Saigon." She returned to the table, and glanced around the room, avoiding Frank's eyes.

"An excitement I don't dwell on much." Frank sipped his coffee. "I know many of the old codgers like to sit around and exaggerate war stories, but not me. I'd be happy if I never thought of those days again."

"I'm terribly sorry I brought back bad memories," said Martha.

"Now Martha, don't go reading me wrong. You brought some beauty and class into our rough military world. Your presence gave us better manners than we might have had otherwise!"

"Oh, yes, I remember the remarks. 'Straighten your tie, Martha's here, clean up your language. Martha might overhear you'" She stood abruptly. "I have to go get ready for the tour."

"I wish you'd stay a bit. I really would like to know more about your writing." Frank gave Martha a sad smile and put his hand on hers.

"Maybe some other time." Martha pulled her hand away as if she'd been burned. She placed her empty cup on the buffet and disappeared down the hall toward the staircase.

"Prickly woman," said Frank. "What's stuck in her craw?" He rubbed his right temple. 'Blasted headache."

As if on cue, Glenda and Isobel came into the dining room as Martha departed. Glenda was dressed in a pink flowered sundress, her pudgy shoulders red from yesterday's sun. She carried a massive straw hat and a large straw purse to match. Isobel's white blouse was tucked neatly into her light blue cotton skirt. She wore a casual denim sun hat with a modest brim.

"A lovely morning to you, ladies." Frank winked at the newcomers. "Ready for another adventure?" He looked pointedly at Glenda's straw bag. "Plan on collecting treasures, I see."

Glenda blushed. "You never know what we might come across today," she said. "Maybe some rare flower seeds. Or a gift shop on Skyline Drive." She opened her blue eyes wide and smiled at Frank.

"Indeed," said Frank. "Now I think I'll have a little more of this excellent coffee, and one of those cherry tarts, then head back to my room to spruce myself up. We'll be off for our Appalachian Wildflower tour within the hour. Should be a great day!"

"I'd like to head home," came a mournful voice from the doorway. Andy Davis glowered at the small gathering in the dining room. "I've had about all of the southern charm and heat I can stand."

"Cheer up, old boy," said Frank. "We're just getting started. I'm sure you'll sing a different tune when we've been to see the mayapples in bloom along Skyline Drive. And our hosts were kind enough to arrange a special tour for us nearby with a local herb expert."

"I won't sing a single note until I'm back in my own apartment," said Andy. He shuffled toward the pile of pastries on the walnut buffet and popped a small blueberry scone into his mouth. "Can't wait to get away from this one-horse town," he added in a muffled voice, spewing small crumbs of scone as he spoke.

"No need to be offensive, my friend." Frank licked his fingers and swept up crumbs of pastry on his plate. "Custer's Mill has a great little history of its own. Part of the Underground Railroad during the Civil War, you know. I read that a tunnel even comes out onto this very property."

Andy walked out of the dining room without answering.

Martha stood at the top of the stairs and looked down over the railing. She had been listening to the conversations below. Now, she watched as Frank started up the wide stairway. Backing away from the railing, she stepped into her room and closed the door. She removed the laptop from her suitcase and placed it on the small desk. A look of calm settled over her face as she adjusted the chair in front of the desk. Her fingers began to move over the familiar keys.

***

The Brubaker tour bus was parked just outside the front door of the Compass Rose Bed & Breakfast. Billy Brubaker sat behind the wheel, tapping his fingers on the dashboard. Serafina watched from an upstairs bedroom window of the mansion and wondered, like many in the town of Custer's Mill, just how Billy felt about his family home being willed to Nanette, Jane, and Marguerite. He almost certainly felt a sense of betrayal when his only living relative snubbed him in her will. Marguerite had warned Serafina last night that Frank had an abrasive personality. Both she and Billy would have to be careful how they responded to Frank's annoying remarks.

Serafina turned back to the carry-all bag she'd packed the night before. Everything seemed in order. It was nice of the ladies to let her stay the night in the attic bedroom at the B&B. But she was doing them a favor as well, being an unofficial guide for today's garden tour. She was sorry she'd gotten up too late to enjoy the delicious breakfast the ladies had prepared. She tidied the comforter on the small, twin bed and closed the door behind her. She heard Frank call out a hearty greeting to Billy and grinned to herself as she saw Billy cringe. Should be an interesting trip.

"Hey everybody!" Serafina smiled at the small group assembling in front of the bus. All turned toward her in unison. The women sized her up in silence, but Andy's and Frank's eyes lit up in appreciation. Serafina was used to the effect she had on men. They all responded in a similar way to her magical manner, ginger hair and petite figure. Sarah nudged Andy. "Quit staring," she whispered, loud enough for everyone to overhear.

"My, what a delightful sight," said Frank. "Who are you, my dear?"

"I'm Serafina Wimsey. Jane asked me to come along with you today. I understand we'll be going up the mountain to Skyline Drive first and then head back over to Bessie's cabin. I'm known as a bit of an expert on flowers and herbs around here. When we get to Jenkin's Hollow, I'll show you around Bessie's old place. I know it like my own backyard, and can show you some of her special mountain plants in the forest around the holler."

"Well, that sounds grand to me, lovely lady. I'll let you be my guide anytime, anywhere." Frank winked.

Glenda nodded shyly to Billy as she climbed the bus steps. Isobel ignored him and they settled into the middle bench seat. Sarah and Andy scowled at Frank and chose seats in the back.

"Where's Martha?" asked Glenda. "She was with us in the foyer."

"Probably powdering her nose," said Frank. "Wouldn't you guess so, Billy Boy?"

Billy shrugged, his smile stretched thin.

Serafina had just settled into the front seat next to Billy when Martha came from around the side of the house to join the group. Frank motioned to her and patted the seat next to him, but Martha chose to squeeze in beside the two sisters, giving Frank the entire first bench to himself.

Billy turned around to face his passengers. "Okay folks, buckle up and we're off."

As they drove along the highway leading to Skyline Drive, it was obvious that spring had arrived late at the higher altitude of the mountaintops. . The line of pale green foliage stopped about halfway up the mountain, leaving the trees and undergrowth at the top of the ridge a stark brown. But once they arrived in Shenandoah National Park, they were treated to grand displays of mayapples thickly carpeting the forest floor. On a short trail walk near the Jewell Hollow Overlook, Serafina pointed out blooming trillium and lady's slippers and even some early blooming mountain laurel.

Serafina's presence was a boon to the group. Even Andy and Isobel set aside their usual snide remarks to make pleasant comments about the flora of the mountains. Thus far, it was a successful outing.

***

Later that afternoon, the van made a slow approach to Bessie Crawford's place. Only Frank and Glenda were still chatting. For the past twenty minutes, the others had grown silent. They hoped to avoid embarrassment and hold onto their lunches as the van bumped and lurched up the washed-out gravel road.

The house came into view around the final bend and Billy parked on the sparse grass at the base of the steep stone walkway. The guests piled out of the van and began taking pictures of the mountain vistas. Serafina unbuckled her seat belt and sat a moment, gazing at the beloved little house. She'd spent many happy hours here with Bessie, learning her potions and plant magic. She missed the old woman.

As she stared at the upstairs window, her stomach twisted and she froze. It couldn't be. Serafina shook her head and ignored the sound of the group tramping toward the old garden area. Her eyes were fixed on the window. Nothing. No one was there. She must have imagined the face.

She shook off a chill and stepped out of the van to join the others. The group stood in the trees downhill from the house, Martha and Glenda were commenting on the variety of plants in the surrounding forest. The others stared at Serafina, impatient for her tour to begin.

"Here's some dogbane." Serafina pointed to a stand of tall branching, plants with deep green leaves. "Also known as flytrap dogbane. The flowers attract flies, then, snap! They bend inward and trap their prey. The milky root is used to slow the pulse but can be tricky to regulate, so you have to be careful with it."

"What's this pretty plant sprouting out of the rocks?" Martha had strayed ahead of the group and stood at the base of the steep bank next to the house. "It's such a nice bright green color."

"Ah, that's not a native, I'm afraid. I brought back some seeds from Europe for Bessie and she let me plant them here." Serafina knelt beside the plant and caressed it with both hands. "This is wild sweet fennel, and it will be covered with lovely yellow flowers in July and August. It's a beautiful plant and useful, too. You can make fennel tea to treat coughs, or use fennel oil from the seeds to make medicine for colicky babies."

"This is celandine poppy or wood poppy," said Serafina. She now led the group to a low-growing cluster of plants next to the forest path. The plants were covered with bright yellow flowers. She snapped a stem and held it up for the group to see the orange sap inside. "This is toxic sap. It's a poppy and has all the properties of California poppies. It needs special handling if you want to use it medicinally. Bessie knew how to make sleep aids out of it. I'm sure there are still some dried poppy roots inside her house. She was a master herbalist, was Bessie. A great loss to those of us who wanted to learn more."

For the next hour, the group asked questions as they strolled through the forest learning the lore and uses of mountain plants. Serafina was careful to keep them away from Marv and Petey's secret tree nursery. No need to stir up questions about those little saplings.

The tour over, everyone headed back to the van. Each person carried one or two samples picked from their walk, quiet and full of their own thoughts. Andy and Sarah walked hand-in-hand, happy to bask in the enchantment of spring that permeated the air in the hollow. Frank had grown blessedly silent during the past half hour or so. Perhaps the mountain views and woodland scents had calmed their earlier irritations. Even Billy was relaxed as he waited in the van, enjoying the warm breeze that ruffled his hair.

Before they pulled away. Serafina craned her neck to take one more look at the upper window. Nothing. It was just that magic she always felt at Bessie's house.

Wednesday Evening

May 29

Jake returned to his house with a few minutes to spare before it was time to head over to Professor Nelson's place. He'd just dropped Kate off at Nanette's farm. Yet again. He needed to find a permanent nanny for his daughter, for her sake and his own. Of course, he was grateful Kate was well-cared for by Nanette and others during the long hours he was working, but he couldn't continue to depend on their generosity. He was disappointed Nanette had turned him down when he asked if she'd be a substitute guardian for Kate. He hoped the Professor would agree, or he'd be back to square one.

He sat on the front steps of his little house and enjoyed the quiet moment. There'd been no time lately to soak in the softness of late May at dusk. The world of jumbled fragrances, echoes, and impressions. All four seasons seemed to be bundled together into one enigmatic freeze frame. The pink pastel sky spoke of springtime and hinted at the promise of summer. Yet the cool northwesterly breeze was a reminder that fall and winter had held center stage just a few weeks ago. Witch weather. Jake had learned that's what the mountain folks around here called it. Weather that confused you. Made you lonesome. Made you long for a place you weren't even sure existed.

He wished his task matched the charm of the evening. That his solemn mission would somehow dissolve into something whimsical and lighthearted. He knew that wouldn't happen. Couldn't happen. But at least he'd enjoy the short drive to Professor Albert Nelson's house. He'd enjoy the fleeting witch weather while he had a couple of minutes to himself.

Jake started his car and his radio blared. He should have turned it off when he came back home after dropping Kate off. The song hit him full force. It really wasn't a romantic song, but it was the tune that was playing the night he first saw Mirabelle. Saw her take off her shoes to dance with a freckle-faced boy. He'd wanted to strangle that boy. To pick him up by the skinny necktie he wore and dangle him in the air until he released the beautiful girl he was holding.

He'd contained his rage until the Eagles had finished singing *Take It to the Limit One More Time.* And then he'd walked over, tapped Mirabelle on the shoulder and motioned her away from her dance partner. She'd looked surprised at first, then giggled and followed him to a corner sofa. He couldn't remember a word they'd said. He just knew he'd fallen in love with the blond-haired, blue-eyed goddess.

And there it was again. The song. If it all fell to pieces tomorrow, would you still be mine? It did fall to pieces. It shattered the night Mirabelle died. And she was still his. He wondered if she took up so much space in his heart that he'd never have room for anyone else. Room for Emma. He sighed and pulled into Professor Nelson's driveway. Known as Uncle Albert to Emma. Great-grandpa to Kate. Other than Billy, he was her closest kin.

Professor Nelson met him at the door. "Come on in, Jake, my boy. I saw a couple of bats swooping down low a while ago. Wouldn't want you to get nipped. Hoyt Miller told me they've already had a few cases of rabies over at Mill City."

Jake followed Albert as he shuffled into his cluttered living room, brushing against the stacks of books and journals that lined the narrow foyer. Albert shooed a smoky gray cat from an upholstered high-backed chair and motioned for Jake to sit.

"Care for tea? That breeze is a little crisp this evening."

"Only if you're drinking some."

"I suppose I could stand another cup. Mia filled me up with chicken potpie and biscuits this evening. I think she's trying to fatten me up a bit. Had to let my belt out a notch or two." He patted his flat stomach and smiled. His wrinkled face and pointed gray beard reminded Jake of a cheerful gnome.

The tea was strong and sweet. Jake held the warm cup in both hands and relaxed. There was something about the hot tea, the cluttered room, and the smiling elderly gentleman that eased the load on Jake's mind. It didn't lift the burden, but it made it lighter. More bearable. He cleared his throat.

"Albert, I've come to see you about an important matter. Something that's been bothering me for a long time now."

The professor leaned closer to Jake. "Sounds serious. How can I help?"

Jake set his cup on a saucer on an end table. "You know, sir, I'm Kate's sole guardian," he said. "Of course, that's as it should be. I'm her father. But lately, I've been thinking. What if something happened to me? I mean, it's not likely I'll be shot in the line of duty here in Custer's Mill, but what if I had an accident? What if I crashed my car? What if I were no longer able to care for Kate?"

"Jake, my boy. Slow down. You're making this old man's head hurt. You're creating disaster too quickly."

"But isn't that how disaster happens? Suddenly? Without warning?" asked Jake. He spoke in a loud, urgent tone, startling the gray cat.

The cat stared at Jake with narrowed eyes. Jake patted the chair beside him, but the cat turned its head as though it had been greatly insulted and stalked back into the kitchen.

"I do understand that it's good to be prepared," said the professor. "But the look on your face as you were talking was quite—how shall I say it? Quite tragic. But life mellows with age, Jake. Oh, we still feel sadness. Sorrow. Pain. But misfortune and heartbreak no longer surprise us. We've learned to expect it. Memento mori."

"Right. Memento mori. Remember that you must die," said Jake. He leaned back into the worn upholstery. "I'm quite aware of death, since my wife, Maribelle, died. But to be honest, I don't like to think about it. I hate death. It's a thief."

Observing the grief etched on the young man's face, the professor regretted his choice of words. "I'm sorry, Jake," he said. "I didn't mean to stir up painful memories." He put his hand on Jake's arm.

"But death is why I'm here, Professor," Jake said. "Please don't apologize. I'm trying to get past these emotional reactions I keep having. It's time." Jake rubbed the back of his neck. "Now, let me tell you why I'm here. I have an important favor to ask you. More than a favor, really."

"Go ahead, my boy. Tell me what's on your mind," said the professor.

"Yes, sir," said Jake. "I want to ask if you to consider becoming Kate's legal guardian in case…well, in case I would die."

The professor peered at Jake over his wire-rimmed glasses. "In case you would die. Of course, the odds are I will die long before you. I've already outlived my promised three-score and ten." Despite his solemn words, the professor's eyes twinkled. He cleared his throat and continued.

"If you'd asked me this question six months ago, I most certainly would have said no. But in the past six months, a miracle has happened."

Jake raised his eyebrows. "A miracle?"

"Yes indeed. A miracle. The lovely Maria Kramer has agreed to be my wife."

"You're marrying Mia?" Jake tried to keep the incredulity out of his voice. Mia had to be at least 15 years younger than Professor Nelson.

"Yes, my boy. I am marrying the angel, Maria. I prefer her beautiful given name. I made a rather fumbling, awkward proposal, but she graciously accepted."

"Congratulations! Mia is quite a catch. Why just her cooking alone would charm most men."

"Ah, but her cooking is only one of her wonderful qualities. She is kind, caring, and most importantly, full of life. She has put joy back into these old bones. Why we even went dancing the other evening!"

Jake rose to shake the old man's hand. "I am so happy. Thrilled for you both."

"Yes, it's much more happiness than I deserve. But now that Maria and I will be husband and wife, I must talk to her about your proposal. It becomes a joint decision, you see. Your request that I…we…would care for Kate in the event of your demise."

"Of course. I completely understand. Talk with her and let me know. I'm especially nervous about Kate's future since she inherited a good portion of the Brubaker estate. One of my greatest fears is—and this may sound unkind—but I don't want Billy Brubaker to intervene. If something happened to me, that is. She's related to him through the Brubaker line."

"Yes, that would concern me too," said the professor. He nodded gravely. "I think Billy has mended his ways somewhat, but he's still not above the temptation of a large fortune. I'll talk to Maria tomorrow and get back with you very soon."

Jake nodded and looked at his watch. "Thank you so much, Albert, for your hospitality and your friendship. And for considering my request about Kate."

"I have many sins on my account, Jake," said the professor. "Not least the sin of abandoning Ruth all those years ago."

"Not one of us is perfect, Albert. We all have regrets," said Jake. "But you're moving on. Just think. You'll soon be a married man!"

"I'd appreciate it if you'd keep that bit of news under your hat for a few days. I know Maria would like to make the announcement. So this is only between us men for now. Deal?"

"It's a deal, Albert. And I'm very happy for you."

The professor walked Jake to the door. "Looks like a storm brewing," he said. "That dark cloud has almost blotted out the moon. You can't trust May weather."

The radio music on the car radio had changed to jazz. Jake tapped his fingers to the beat as he drove the back roads to Nanette's farm. Jazz was safe. He had no memories associated with jazz. The dark cloud now completely covered the half moon that had just appeared on the horizon. A fat drop of rain splashed on the windshield. The witch weather was dissolving into a typical late spring evening. Jake sighed. *Memento mori.*

***

Terri cleared away the remains of the evening meal and stacked the dishes on the counter. The guests had raved about the meal. A delectable fragrance of perfectly roasted pork, garlic potatoes and green beans with toasted almonds still perfumed the air in the kitchen.

Hot, sudsy water steamed in the sink. She tied an apron behind her back and donned a pair of rubber gloves. She picked up a metal scrubber, plunged the large broiler pan into the water, and began to scrub with a vengeance.

"You're not a teenager, so quit moping around like one," she muttered to herself. "Keep your mind on your chores. He's not interested."

She was still elbow-deep in the dishwater ten minutes later when her phone rang. As quickly as she could, she began to pull off the rubber gloves. "Don't hang up, don't hang up, get off, you stupid gloves!"

One glove remained obstinately stuck on her hand. With a loud snap she yanked it off inside out, and grabbed her phone.

"Hello?"

"Hello, Terri, this is Laurence. I hope I'm not catching you at an inconvenient time. You sound a bit out of breath."

Terri smiled. "Not at all, Laurence. Just cleaning up after dinner and glad to take a break." She settled herself into a chair at the kitchen table with a happy grin on her face.

***

Marguerite, Jane and Nanette had invited their guests to join them in the parlor. They intended to facilitate some pleasant after-dinner conversation and possibly even a game of charades. The little group settled into seats around the room.

Only Andy remained standing. He studied two bottles of wine on the barley twist side table, which also held several leaded crystal wine glasses. He held a bottle up to the group with a questioning look. "Any takers? "he asked. "Merlot or Chardonnay."

"Yes, if you're pouring." Said Frank. His face was pale and his eyes looked clouded. "That merlot looks like a good, smooth choice. The red we had with dinner tasted a bit acidic to me. And I'm feeling the need for something a bit stronger, but wine will do."

Andy poured two glasses of wine and handed one to Frank. He sat down next to Sarah, muttering something indecipherable under his breath.

"Didn't quite catch what you said, Andy," said Frank. "I'm sure it was uplifting, though."

"You have such a knack for rubbing people the wrong way, Frank," said Andy. "A real magic touch." Sarah put her hand on Andy's thigh and gave him a warning look.

"Not to worry, Sarah." Frank gave the couple a brief bow. "Andy's crankiness is no skin off my teeth." He rubbed his hands together and looked at Marguerite. "By the way, you ladies might consider calling in an exterminator."

"Why whatever for?" asked Jane. "Nanette? Marguerite? We haven't had any pesky bug problems, have we?"

"Nah, I mean to get rid of the magpies." Frank looked pointedly at the Fischer sisters.

The proprietresses of the B&B looked even more confused. "Magpies?" they said almost in unison.

"Yeah, you know. Those birds that steal shiny trinkets and things?"

Glenda glanced at her sister and hurriedly looked away.

"Couple of things missing from the place," said Frank.

"Missing? What things? Was something taken from your room?" Jane moved closer to Frank.

"Not only my room. Martha said her Cross pen set was not on her desk where she put it. My Vietnam Randall attack knife is not in my suitcase either." Frank got up to refill his wine glass.

"Why in heaven's name would you bring an attack knife on a garden tour?" Isobel stared at Frank. She looked genuinely surprised.

"A buddy of mine who lives in Richmond wanted to see it. He's interested in buying it off me."

"I think it's a bad idea to carry around weapons," said Isobel.

"Apparently it was a dumb move on my part. And my knife isn't simply a weapon. It's a handy tool for lots of things. Didn't expect it to be pinched right from under my nose, though."

"I'm sure you just misplaced it," said Jane. She felt a flutter of anxiety in her chest. "We have a very safe little town here."

"I'll bet there are other things missing, too," Frank continued as though Jane hadn't spoken at all. "Maybe you'd better call that young police chief of yours to come and take a look around. Or maybe," he added with a smirk, "you need to get rid of the magpies."

"I think it's time to talk about something more enlightening." Marguerite's tone was severe and her blue eyes bored into Frank. "What's on your agenda for tomorrow?"

Frank stood up. "Oh, I see, changing the subject. Well. Sorry if my chit-chat wasn't up to your high standards, madam. I shall leave you to your high-class conversation. I'm going outside to clear my fuzzy head. Too much wine, I guess," he said. He winked and walked unsteadily out the door to the porch.

"My, my, he's tipsy, isn't he?" Nanette shook her head. "Well, next time we'll have to keep track of how much our guests have imbibed. Live and learn."

Jane looked defeated, and Marguerite's face was unreadable.

Martha was still smiling, and Andy and Sarah had perked up at Frank's unsteady exit. The sisters, Glenda and Isobel, excused themselves to their room.

After five more minutes of stiff, uncomfortable small talk, the remainder of the group disbursed. The ladies headed into the kitchen to debrief and commiserate about their difficult evening. This was not the kind of interaction they'd pictured when they talked about opening Bertha's home as a bed & breakfast.

"Maybe we need to read up on group ice breakers," said Jane. "You know, fun little questions so folks can get to know each other better. This group is a bit icy, for sure."

"Cheer up, Jane," said Nanette." At least we'll have this group of pilgrims just one more day. Now let's wash up those wine glasses and go home. Terri is in her room here if they need anything else tonight. Let's remember to remind her to lock up and keep these wackos off the streets of our town." She snorted.

All three ladies looked at each other, then broke into uncontrollable giggles.

Thursday Morning

May 30

The scent of bacon floated into the elegant dining room. The garden tour guests had gathered around the linen-covered walnut table, carefully set with Bertha Brubaker's Royal Doulton china, complete with matching tea and coffee pots. Their bags and suitcases sat in the large entry hall, ready to be loaded into the tour bus. The group was heading for eastern Virginia today and new accommodations. This was to be their last impression of the Compass Rose Bed & Breakfast, and the ladies intended to make it a great one.

Jane and Marguerite were hard at work in the spacious kitchen, placing garnishes on plates of eggs benedict made with eggs gathered fresh at Nanette's farm that morning. Nanette was arranging a crystal bowl of mint-infused fruit salad at the counter.

"I'll drain this bacon and arrange it on a plate, Jane," said Marguerite. "I think we're ready to serve everything. Let's get it out there while the eggs are hot." She picked up a fork and began to arrange the bacon in neat rows.

Hiram sat at the end of the kitchen table, eating his usual—oatmeal, no sugar, with a few raisins sprinkled in for sweetness. He glanced up at Jane and slowly shook his head. "Ain't healthy for folks to eat that kind of food first thing in the morning. You should be giving them some good hot cereal like this here." He waved a spoon full of oatmeal around, dropping a blob on the table.

"Well, Hiram, we want to be known for great breakfasts and elegant rooms. Oatmeal isn't fancy enough for our guests. I know you think plain is better, but it's fun to offer special recipes and watch people enjoy them. One of our guests, Frank Wright, told me breakfast was his favorite meal of the day. And I'm sure he's not expecting cereal."

Hiram grunted and scooped up the errant bit of oatmeal on his forefinger. He licked it off and turned back to his bowl.

"At any rate, I need to go and find Mr. Wright so he can join us for the meal," said Jane. "He must be outside, taking in the garden before breakfast."

The old screen door swung wide, then banged shut behind her. Jane jumped, then turned and poked her head back into the kitchen.

"Hiram, I keep forgetting to ask you to work on this door sometime," she said. "I hate when it slams like that."

Hiram nodded in silent acknowledgment, and she stepped back outside.

The wind whipped up sharply and she covered her head with her hands to avoid a complete disaster with her coiffure. She passed the rose garden and walked as fast as she could toward the wooden Adirondack chairs under the spreading maple tree where she had last seen Frank. His hat was perched on a chair, but he was not in sight. Large drops of rain began to spatter down through the tree. She stopped and glanced back toward the veranda of the mansion, but no one sat there either. She called out across the lawn. "Mr. Wright. Your favorite meal is ready to serve. Everyone is at the table, so if you're ready..."

No answer. Jane jogged back to the kitchen, and glanced around the lawn one more time for a glimpse of her wayward guest. Breakfast must be served now. They'd have to put some food aside for Frank to eat when he reappeared.

"Did you find him? You're wet!" said Marguerite. She held a tray of steaming plates. "We need to get this food served now."

"A storm's coming up," said Jane. She dried her hands on a towel and fluffed her hair. "No, I didn't, but let's go ahead and serve everyone else. We'll have to make him a plate later when he shows up. Kind of thoughtless for the leader, I should think, but oh well. If he's out walking, he's going to get caught in a downpour."

Jane and Marguerite greeted their guests cheerfully as they served the eggs and bacon. Nanette followed with the crystal bowl of fruit salad and a large basket of warm, fragrant croissants. "These eggs came fresh from my farm this morning, folks," said Nanette. "Fresh eggs taste best from happy chickens! And I keep my chickens very happy."

"Wow, great service! Everything looks wonderful," said Martha, reaching for a hot roll. But where's our fearless leader? I know he loves big breakfasts."

Jane looked at Marguerite, then back at Martha. "We're not sure. I haven't seen him this morning yet. I'm sure he'll be along shortly."

"No great loss there," said Andy. "Disappearing is part of his M-O. Or making someone else's hard-earned cash disappear, that is." Sarah elbowed Andy under the table.

"He's probably hiding," said Isobel. "His drinking last night was shameful. Sleeping it off somewhere, no doubt." She sniffed. "But enough about him. Let's eat while it's hot. By the way, these dishes are beautiful, Miss White. Quite rare, I believe."

"Our benefactor and friend, Bertha Brubaker, left us not only the house, but all the furnishings, including her world-class china collection."

"Quite a windfall for you, I should think," said Isobel. Her eyes opened wide as she speared a chunk of English muffin underneath her eggs and popped it into her mouth. The dual actions made her face look strange and slightly maniacal.

The ladies left their guests to their meal and returned to the kitchen. Rain and wind lashed against the large windows facing the garden. "We should call Jake now to look into Frank Wright's whereabouts," said Marguerite. "I'm getting worried. We haven't seen him since last night. Maybe Terri will know if he came in before she locked up. I told her to take this morning off, though, we're just doing breakfast today."

"He's just lollygagging somewhere. Taking a break from his friendly tour group. No need to bother our town police over it." Nanette sat at the kitchen table, drying pots and pans with an old striped linen cloth.

"She's right, Nanette. This is strange," said Jane. "It's raining and he's still outside. Plus, the group is supposed to head out of here at 10:00. That's only an hour from now." Jane looked out the door across the lawn, hoping for a glimpse of Frank. "If Jake doesn't want to do anything, that's his prerogative, but we need to at least let him know."

"Very well, have it your way." Nanette draped the towel over the back of a metal chair. "But I say you're making this into a tempest in a teapot."

***

Jake and his deputy, Jason Dove, had spent twenty minutes walking around the large Compass Rose property in the growing storm. It was a good thing they'd donned their yellow slickers and boots back at the station. Jake had agreed to take a look when Jane called, although he expected that Frank Wright would show up on his own, especially in this weather. As time passed, his concern increased.

"I'm going down to the little creek there behind the old wooden fence. There's a trail along that creek, and maybe he went there for a walk. You keep looking around here, Dove, then head down Rosemary Street and ask around at nearby houses."

Jake crunched through old leaves and sticks to reach a faint trail beside the small stream. As he rounded a bend, he could see a man leaning against the trunk of a tree, his feet propped up against a large rotting log.

"Mr. Wright?" he called out, but received no response. He stopped and blinked. Was he ignoring him on purpose? Was he sound asleep? Or worse?

Jake increased his speed and moved around the tree so he could see Frank's face.

Frank was leaning to the left, causing his navy-blue sport coat to flop open. Water dripped off his head, and a blood stain blotted the front of his light blue shirt. The fabric looked cut. Jake's insides tightened.

The man's head rested on the tree, his mouth slightly open. His eyes were closed. Jake touched his hand. It was cold. He quickly felt for a pulse, but there was no response. Jake sighed. Frank Wright was dead.

***

Not many people would have seen the tell-tale signs, but Hiram knew someone had used his fishing spot. He'd memorized every twig and branch; practically knew the place of each leaf and acorn shell. Even allowing for the natural movement of wind and rain, he could tell somebody else had stood in his space. Caught perch from his fishing hole. Watched thick-bodied bass from his vantage point. He pulled the hood of his rain poncho over his eyes. The thin plastic didn't keep out much, but it was better than being hit in the face with the slanting rain.

Fishing in a downpour wasn't pleasant, but it usually yielded great results. He didn't own this land, but for years, he'd fished here. Alone. Or sometimes with his grandson. But now, somebody was moving in on his territory. Taking his space. If all went as planned, today would be the day he'd find out who.

He set up his camp stool and dumped the small bowl of wriggling worms into a bucket filled with dirt. He'd let the little critters get some enjoyment out of their last hour or so. He never liked stringing the worms on his hook. If they weren't by far the best trout bait this side of the Mason-Dixon line, he'd never use them. But Hiram was a fisherman first and an environmentalist second.

He cast his first line, then he heard it. There was a rustle behind him. Not a light sound such as a deer might make, or even the rhythmic spattering of raindrops, but the heavy, plodding noise of a human moving through the mud and brush. He reeled his line in a few feet to let it sink into a deep spot of the river and propped his pole on a rock. He wasn't afraid, but he was wary. Over four decades of hard living had given him a keen sense of caution.

Hiram saw the man at least half a minute before the trespasser realized anyone else was nearby. And by the time the stranger saw Hiram, the older man had already stood up and was assessing him with a shrewd gaze.

The newcomer was a tall young man with olive skin and sable-colored eyes. His dark hair was wet with rain and hung in his face. He wore a dark rain slicker, torn a little at the shoulder and the hood had slipped down off his head. The man moved cautiously, like a hunted animal, and looked at Hiram with distrust. He glanced around at the thick brush behind and the flowing water ahead and seemed to realize that he had no choice but to acknowledge Hiram's presence.

"Hello," he said cautiously.

Hiram nodded.

"Rough weather, is it not? Have you caught anything?" the young man said. He leaned his fishing pole against a tree and slid his backpack on to the wet leaves. He relaxed slightly when he realized that Hiram wasn't about to run him off the property.

Hiram shook his head. "Just got here."

"I caught a couple of sun perch and a trout yesterday. But I came a lot earlier in the morning. It must be getting close to noon by now. I hoped the storm would let up, but by the look of the clouds it will rain all day." The man spoke with an accent that Hiram couldn't quite place. "Do you fish here often?"

Hiram scowled. "This is my spot. Too crowded here now."

The young man looked puzzled. "Only you and me, from what I can tell," he said. He squinted and looked down the river as if expecting to see a multitude of people tramping over the rocks. "My name is David."

Hiram grunted.

"Do you live near the river?" asked David, squatting down to tie a spinner on the end of his line. When Hiram didn't answer, David continued, "I'm only passing through. I thought I'd camp out a few nights and then move on."

Hiram sensed tension in the young man's voice. Something about the tone. Too light. Too casual. Too fast. Hiram didn't trust fast talkers.

"You do not talk much, do you?" David released the line and both men watched the silver bait glisten as it arched over the water and landed near Hiram's spot.

"In the multitude of words there wanteth not sin," said Hiram, reeling his line back in and throwing it off to the side away from David's cast.

"Pardon? Are you some kind of Shakespeare scholar?" said David.

"King James version of the Holy Bible." Hiram looked disgusted at David's lack of scripture knowledge.

"Are you a priest or something?"

Hiram shook his head slowly. "Where you camping at?"

David looked up sharply as if the sudden shift in topics had thrown him off guard. He gestured vaguely toward the area behind him. "Back there. In the national forest."

"Lines are blurred here. Hard to tell national forest from Bessie Crawford's land. She owned 129 acres all the way through here." Hiram made a wide sweep with one arm as if including all visible and invisible land for miles around.

David flushed and turned his face away. But not before Hiram saw the change in the young man's countenance.

"Lying lips are an abomination to the Lord," Hiram said. He looked first at David then at his line bobbing the brown-green river.

"Can you just talk in regular English so I can understand?" David was getting agitated under Hiram's intense scrutiny.

When Hiram said nothing, the young man continued. "It's like you know something about me. But we have never met before, have we?"

Hiram still didn't answer but continued to look at David. The rain had slackened to a drizzle, but the wind had picked up, blowing the fishing line in a zigzagging path down the river.

David suddenly stood up and reeled his line back in. "You're a strange man, sir. I will move on and allow you to fish alone," he said. He attached the fishing hook to an eye on the pole and hoisted his wet backpack onto his shoulder.

"Sit down," said Hiram. He pointed to a large fallen log.

David hesitated, but he let his backpack slide down his arm.

"Sit and talk," said Hiram, his voice soft but firm. He pulled his line in, careful to dodge a branch swirling downstream. He gave David an even stare and waited.

David looked out over the water to the bank on the other side. Neither man spoke for a several moments, but the silence wasn't uncomfortable—at least not for Hiram. The older man picked up a river rock and began examining a small fossil embedded on its flat surface.

"Are you some kind of medicine man?" said David finally. He sat down on the log. "I don't understand. How can you make me talk when you do not say anything yourself?"

Hiram twisted his wrist and skimmed the stone across the agitated water. It seemed to dodge the current and made seven skips before it finally sank to the bottom.

"I am impressed," said David. "I can only do four. I could not skip a stone at all in this wind and rain."

Hiram picked up another pebble and began to wipe it on his pant leg.

"I'm not camping, you know," said David.

Hiram grunted.

"I'm not even in this country legally, he said. His voice was defiant. "There. I said it. Call the authorities. I do not care. I am illegal, but that is no worry now. My sorrows are greater than that."

Hiram fastened clear blue eyes on the young man. "Why are you here?"

"The great Sphinx speaks," said David with a wry smile.

Hiram frowned.

"Why am I here?" said David. "That is an excellent question, but here I am without an excellent answer." His expressive hands made sweeping motions through the air.

Hiram pulled out a small bag of split shot and began threading the little metal ball on to his fishing line. He worked slowly and methodically, his actions soothing and familiar to the young man.

"All right." David said. He slapped both hands down on his knees. "You win. I am here because of a woman. A woman who has haunted me for a long time now. She will not leave me in peace. She appears in every tune I play on my violin; sabotages every thought I have for the future. There. Are you happy? I have told you my troubles."

"Serafina?"

Hiram's one-word question was spoken softly, but to David it seemed as though the old man had shouted it from one end of the Shenandoah River to the other.

"You know her?" asked David. "Well isn't that a silly question? Of course, you do. What man within 3,000 miles doesn't know her? Yes. Serafina."

Hiram nodded.

"I was married to her once, you know. She was my wood sprite. Magical. Beautiful." David paused as if he expected Hiram to show some sort of surprise at his statement. When he said nothing, David continued. "She lived with us for three years. 'Us' meaning my people. The Romani."

"I know," said Hiram, once more casting his line into a quiet pool at the edge of the river.

"Did she tell you?" asked David. "I am shocked. I thought I would be the last person she'd talk about. It was all a crazy mix-up. I had to be away for a while, and she suspected the worst. Women always do that, you know. Suspect the worst. When I came back, she was gone. Gone without a message. Without a trace."

"She didn't tell me," said Hiram. "Figured it out." He pulled sharply on his pole and both men watched as a rainbow trout struggled against the hook in its mouth. Hiram reeled in the line, gently unhooked the fish, and threw it back into the water.

"Why did you throw it back?" said David. "That would have made a delicious meal." He looked at the old man with a mixture of surprise and contempt. "Do you not eat the fish you catch?"

"When I'm hungry," said Hiram, baiting his hook again, this time with salmon eggs.

"Well, I'm hungry," said David. "If I don't catch fish, I don't eat."

"Why are you here?" Hiram said again as if David's first answer didn't satisfy his curiosity.

"I told you. I'm here because I can't get Serafina out of my head. She's set up a tent there or something. I need to see her in person, but I am afraid."

"What are you going to do?"

"I don't know," said David. "I need some time to figure out a way to talk to her. To let her know I'm here without making her run away. Those old men—Marv and Petey Blue—said I could stay in their aunt's cabin for a while if I...took care of the place." David stopped, suddenly remembering the secrecy surrounding the American chestnut trees he was asked to guard.

"Truth always wins," said Hiram reeling in another trout. This time he unhooked the fish and handed it to David. "For supper," he said.

"Much obliged, sir," said David, hooking the still squirming fish onto a small metal stringer. "Are you going to tell anybody I'm here?"

Hiram looked up at a tall sycamore tree growing next to the river, its roots sunk deep into the sandy loam. When he spoke, his voice was quiet and David had to strain to hear him. "You shall know the truth, and the truth will set you free."

Thursday Morning

May 29

"Oooooo!" squealed Glenda, as she pulled her tight blue flowered dress over her chubby knees. The mauve colored wing chair was charming as an Edwardian period piece, but it didn't suit Glenda's short, stocky build. Her feet hovered an inch above the floor and the narrow sides pinched her full hips. "It's just like the Agatha Christie books!" she said. "All of us here in the library, waiting for Hercule Poirot to come in, twirl his moustaches and start the questioning. And it's even dark and rainy outside." She gave a delighted giggle.

Isobel glared at her sister. "Get hold of yourself, Glenda! First of all, this is not England, and the young policeman I saw in the foyer is no Poirot." She pulled a book from a lower shelf of one of the dark, old bookcases and began to rifle through the pages absently.

Glenda's lips puckered into a pout. "You're no fun at all, sister. You never were good at playing imagination games."

"This is no game, ladies," snapped Martha.

Andy and Sarah sat in a corner. Both looked straight ahead, not acknowledging the other guests' presence in the room. Sarah wore a dark maroon tunic with black leggings. Her hair was pulled back into a severe knot at the nape of her neck. Andy's white cotton shirt was wrinkled and his jeans were worn thin around the knees. His sandy brown hair stuck out in a cowlick on the right side of his head. They both looked very young.

As a whole, the group appeared shocked when they heard of Frank's death, but none of them seemed particularly distressed at the grim news.

All heads turned as the door to the library opened and Police Chief Jake Preston and his deputy, Jason Dove, walked in.

"Good morning, folks," said Jake. He looked around the room at the motley gathering.

Only Glenda gave him a dimpled smile and patted her curly grey hair. "Hello there, Detective."

"Police Chief, ma'am. And this is Deputy Dove."

Glenda turned her smile toward Jason. "Why you're only a boy."

"Twenty-three, ma'am," said Jason. He blushed and wished he hadn't spoken. Why did he feel the need to prove himself to people like her?

Glenda put her hand over her mouth. "Why, he reminds me of Wilhelm, sister. Don't you think so?" Her voice trailed off as her sister scowled at her.

"Glenda," said Isobel, "stop this foolish talk at once."

Jake pulled a mahogany-colored chair from a table by the window and motioned for Jason to do the same. "I'll be meeting with each of you individually later on," said Jake. "But right now, I simply want to get a little information about your tour and how you were connected with the deceased."

"A ball and chain," muttered Andy. "We were connected by a ball and chain."

Jake raised an eyebrow. Jason pulled out a notebook and began to write down Andy's words. "Do you want to elaborate, Mr. Davis?" Jake asked.

"Andy. My name is Andy."

"Okay, Andy, would you like to tell me what you mean?" said Jake.

Andy clamped his mouth tightly shut and shook his head.

Martha spoke up. "They were caught up in one of Frank's get rich schemes. One of his many projects that didn't quite work out."

Andy gave Martha a withering glance. He crossed his arms and turned his back on the group without another word.

"And you, ma'am? How did you know Frank?" Jake asked, looking at Martha.

She set her coffee mug down on a little end table by her chair and stared past Andy into the rose hedge visible outside. "How did I know Frank?" said Martha. She spoke softly, as though talking to herself. "How did I know Frank?" she repeated.

Jason moved restlessly, pencil poised, ready to write. Jake relaxed in his chair, smiled at Martha, and said, "Just take your time, ma'am. Like I said, we'll talk to you all individually later. If you'd rather wait until we're alone, that's okay too."

"Well, you're easy enough to get along with," said Martha. She turned her attention back to Jake. A sudden, bright smile lit up her face. "I knew Frank a long time ago. We were in 'Nam together. But that was a world away. A lifetime away. Yes. A lifetime away." Her voice faded, and her eyes wandered back to the garden.

"Do any of you know who might have a motive to kill Frank?" Jake turned from Martha to face the rest of the group. "You have the advantage of knowing him better than I do. Of course, I'll conduct a thorough investigation, but any information you can give me now would be helpful."

"We just met him on this garden tour," said Isobel. "I'm hardly qualified to comment on his enemies. Or his friends for that matter."

"Have you been on other garden tours?" asked Jake.

"I've been on half a million, it seems," said Martha. "I write the garden column for the Chronicle. *The New York Chronicle*, that is. As well as freelance garden articles and any other subjects editors want me to write about."

"You must find that a challenging occupation. Have you traveled with Frank on other occasions?"

"Not on his tour group," said Martha. "I rode shotgun a couple of times back in 'Nam."

"Will you stop talking about the war!" Isobel's outburst was loud and unexpected.

Martha's eyes widened. "Well, pardon me," she said. "Sorry if I offended you. I'm merely answering this officer's questions, you know."

"I'm not offended," said Isobel stiffly. "I just don't like living in the past. We cannot make progress if we are held up by things that happened long ago."

"Yes ma'am," said Martha. She gave Isobel a little salute. "I'll save my war stories for later. Since you're so sensitive. Sorry Chief Preston, can't say any more in her presence." She nodded toward Isobel, who pursed her lips in disapproval.

Jake stood up and motioned for Jason to follow him to the cruiser parked outside. "We're not going to get anything more from this group effort," said Jake quietly. "We'll have to talk to them one by one."

But the morning had not been wasted. Jake hoped forensics would turn up something down by the creek. There's was a definite charge in the air and he was willing to bet that every person on the tour was hiding something. It was up to him to sort through their truths, half-truths and lies. And to figure out if one of them had motive, means and opportunity to kill Frank Wright.

Thursday Midday

May 30

Jane Allman carried a stack of clean towels, pausing on the landing at the top of the stairs. The murder and subsequent upheaval at the mansion had shaken her usual calm outlook.

"You need to focus," she told herself. "Deep breaths, eyes closed. Calm and peace."

When she opened her eyes, she took a few moments to gaze down the long hallway and admire the intricate crown moulding that outlined the ceiling. A hand-braided runner in peach and green ran the length of the old oak floors. The pristine white doors with glass doorknobs leading to each guest bedroom provided a pleasing contrast with the pale, green walls.

Two large palladium windows at the end of the hallway provided a wide view of the front lawn and the circular drive below. Wind whipped through the branches of the trees and rain slatted against the glass. Jane tucked the stack the towels under her arm and bent to straighten the arrangement of baby's breath and rosebuds sitting on an ornate wooden table next to the window.

"Aunt Jane, what are you doing? You look deep in thought. Do you need help with those towels?"

Jane jumped, and turned to face her niece. "Oh, Terri, you startled me! I almost dropped these towels. No, I was just gathering my thoughts and admiring the beauty of this old house. Marv and Petey Blue did a great job on painting."

"We're lucky Jacob Craun sold us any paint at all," said Terri with a wink. "He was so exasperated with Nanette. After he tried to mix the right color several times, and she still wasn't satisfied, he told her she should go somewhere else to get her paint."

Jane laughed. "Yes, but eventually they both cooled down, and Jacob found the right color combination. Even Nanette agreed that he'd managed to create the exact color of green she had in mind.

"But you're right. Petey Blue and Marv have done a decent job of helping to fix up the place," remarked Terri. "Not only can they paint, but their plumbing skills have been a huge blessing, too."

"We had no idea how handy they would be when we hired them," said her aunt. "I miss having them around. Marv with his solemn, silent ways and Petey Blue with his tall tales and silly grin. Still, it's nice the work is finished and ready for guests, with new paint and piping and everything in order."

"Speaking of order. I'd better get back downstairs and finish what I was doing. With all this uproar, we need to do our best to keep things in order and manage our guests." Terri took two steps down the stairs and turned toward her aunt. "Are you sure you don't need any help with those towels?"

"Go on, you," her aunt scoffed. "I'm finished except for replacing these towels in the Katherine room."

“Okay, then.” Terri gave her aunt a small wave and ran down the steps.

Jane turned toward the door of the Katherine Room where Andy and Sarah Davis were staying. Like all the guest rooms in the inn, each door held a brass name plate bearing the name of a former member of the Brubaker family. It was Marguerite’s idea, and they’d all thought it a fitting way to honor their old friend.

Jane’s hand was poised to knock on the door before entering when loud and angry voices came from inside the room. The young Davis couple was having an argument. Jane paused for a moment to listen.

“Did you do it, Andy?” Sarah said. Her tone was accusing.

“What? How could you think such a thing?” said Andy. “Great, now my own wife thinks I’m a murderer.”

“So where’d you go last night?” Sarah asked. “I woke up around two a.m., and you weren’t here. What am I supposed to think? You hated him.” She paused. “Well, to be fair, we both did.”

“Yeah, and I have to say I’m not really sorry he’s dead,” said Andy. His angry response was punctuated with three loud thumps. “But he’s still wreaking havoc because now you don’t trust me.”

Sarah said something undistinguishable. Stomping footsteps inside the room made Jane move down the hallway so she wouldn’t be caught eavesdropping. Her heart pounded in her ears. She strained to hear further conversation from her more distant position. A scraping chair and a feminine cough reassured her that Sarah was still safe. Andy rushed out of the room, slamming the door behind him. He glared at Jane as he passed her. He ran down the stairs and disappeared into the dining room.

Jane grabbed the railing to steady herself. Her face was ashen.

“Aunt Jane?” Terri stood in the hallway below, looking up at her aunt. Her brown tailored slacks and a cream-colored blouse showed off her slim frame. A delicate silver chain decorated with a single pearl adorned her neck.

"Aunt Jane! You still have those towels in your hand. Are you okay? You don't look okay. "

Jane shook her head as if to clear it. "I'm fine, dear. I'll do the Katherine room when the Davises are gone. Andy just went out, but his wife is still in the room."

"By the way, Aunt Jane," said Terri. "In spite of everything that's happened, I was able to find an hour this morning to catch up on the books and pay bills. And did you notice the dust that's collected on the sideboard and some of the tables? While no one was downstairs, I did a quick dusting throughout the rooms. This old furniture collects dust in all the ornate carvings and crevices. Wish we could hire someone to clean this place."

"Well, since you do the books, my dear, you know what our profit margins are. I'm afraid that until we get more guests, we are the help. And with this ...um...current situation, I don't know if the guests who've booked rooms in the coming weeks will still want to stay here."

"I know." Terri said. "It's tough." She hefted her brown leather bag over her shoulder. "And don't think I'm ungrateful for what you, Nanette and Marguerite have done for me. I love staying here at the B&B and helping all of you. And I want to do whatever I can to get us through this rough patch. Really, I do. It's just that cleaning toilets and changing beds isn't what I thought I would be doing with my life."

"Do you think any of us saw this in our future?" Jane asked. "But enough of that. You look like you're headed out. Where are you off to, and it is okay with Jake if you leave the house?"

"Yes, I talked to Jason Dove, and cleared it with him. We have this houseful of hungry, irritated guests that we need to feed for the next who-knows-how-long." Terri opened her bag and retrieved her car keys. "I have to get to Glen's Market for more food. I'll get some fixings for sandwiches for lunch today, and then something for dinner. I think we have enough supplies for breakfast tomorrow, if Nanette can bring us more fresh eggs."

"Sounds good. I'll let the guests know lunch will be a little late, maybe by 1 p.m. or so?"

"That works." Terri smiled at her aunt and waved as she turned to leave.

Jane walked back to the palladium windows and watched Terri pull out of the driveway. Balancing the towels on one arm, she opened the door to the linen closet, and tucked them away on the deep shelves. Then she headed to the kitchen to call Emma and tell her what she'd overheard.

Thursday Afternoon

May 30

"Man! That wind is something else!" Jason stood against the heavy metal door of the police station, and held it back for Jake to enter.

"You got that right!" agreed Jake. He pulled off his dripping hat and coat and hung them on a hook inside the door. "The weather is so unpredictable this time of year. You don't know if you're going to need the heater or the air conditioner."

Jason glanced at a large bulletin board with notices blown askew from the strong blast. "Just had the door open a couple of seconds and already these Most Wanted pictures are all over the place." He began to straighten the papers on the board. "Do they ever catch any of these guys? Or is all for show?"

"I suspect they nab a few." Jake looked at the gathering clouds. Tree branches shook in the heavy gusts and rain drops spattered on the window. "Good thing this old building is sturdy. Guy on TV even mentioned the possibility of a tornado or two, although those TV weather people tend to blow things out of proportion now and then. No pun intended."

The Custer's Mill police station was part of a larger collection of municipal offices housed in the town's former high school. The old brick Federal-style building had been modernized on the inside, but still displayed much of its old-fashioned charm.

The police department was on the right of the main entrance. Large glass windows had been set in the original walls so officers could see who was coming and going. An old glass transom above the oak door was etched in black lettering that read Custer's Mill Police. Jason and two junior officers occupied the front room. A short hallway led to Jake's office at the rear of the building. Two holding cells near Jake's office were not in use often except for the occasional drunk driver.

Jake picked up a pen and twirled it absently. "Glad the forensics team finished up before the storm."

"Yeah. A piece of luck there."

Jason watched his boss. Jake was never one to waste words, but he seemed unusually quiet this afternoon. "Anything wrong?" he asked, as he moved over to his desk and turned on his computer.

Jake grinned. "You know me pretty well, don't you?"

Jason nodded. "Well when you do that twirly thing with your ink pen and stare into space, I know something's running through your head."

"Nanette tells me that she can see my emotions scroll across my face like a marquee. Not sure I like that. It's one thing to be expressive, but transparency might not be a great quality for a police chief."

"I wouldn't worry about it, boss." Jason said. "What's up?"

"It's probably my overactive imagination, but something is not sitting well. Something about those interviews that seems well—sketchy."

"Yeah, nobody wanted to admit they knew the victim very well. But I wonder." Jason said.

Jake put the pen back on the Jason's desk. "So, here's what we have so far. He counted on his fingers. "The woman, Martha, knew him in Vietnam. The young man, Andy Davis, said he was connected to Frank by a 'ball and chain'. Wonder what he meant by that exactly? And that's all we have to go on so far. Unless forensics comes up with a weapon. And until I hear back from Atkins."

Jason nodded. "Yep. Definitely some bad blood between Davis and the deceased. But it's nothing we can build a case on. Not yet, certainly."

"You're right there. I think we'll start with the victim. Who was this Frank Wright? Who wanted him dead?" Jake walked toward the back hall. "Think I'll give Atkins a call, see if he's got anything for us yet. I know it looks pretty obvious. Guy was taking a walk and somebody stabbed him, but you know Atkins. He always seems to find helpful details we may have missed."

***

Jason sat down at his desk and turned on the old computer. He'd hoped the budget would allow him to get a newer one like Jakes this year, but it didn't look like that was going to happen. The dinosaur of a machine was as slow as molasses in wintertime. At least the town had put cable internet in the building after a couple of town employees threatened to quit if they didn't get rid of DSL. One day soon, that would be as obsolete as old telephone party lines, he was sure.

The screen finally opened and Jason typed "Frank Wright, Marine," in the search bar. The modem started to grind with the weight of the search, but eventually, a list of options popped up. Jason clicked on a short announcement from a Northern Virginia daily newspaper. It was dated June 1, 1995, and accompanied by a photo of a younger Frank decked out in full Marine uniform. Jason squinted at the small print under the photograph.

The Falls Church Veterans Association honors retiring Marine Captain Frank J. Wright. Basic training at Quantico where Frank entered into Officer Candidate School ...First deployment in 1971 as a Second Lieutenant to the DMZ in South Korea.... He earned the rank of First Lieutenant and a Purple Heart after one year in Vietnam at the end of the conflict, 1972-1973 .... After serving tours in Beirut, Persian Gulf, and Afghanistan he rose to the rank of Captain.

"Well would you look at that!" Jason whistled at the list of accolades. "With all the times he put his life on the line he ended up dying on a woodland trail in Custer's Mill. Kind of ironic."

The article was long with several embedded links. Jason could see the danger of rabbit-trailing on the enticing paths. However, one link caught his eye. An article about upcoming troop withdrawals written by war correspondent, Martha Stanton. Martha Stanton. Now there was a familiar name. According to the article, Wright and his men were among the last Marines to leave Saigon. They had the challenging responsibility to help get all diplomats out of harm's way and back home to safety. Second Lieutenant Frank Wright had been injured during the evacuation.

Miss Stanton had written a good PR piece for the Marines during a difficult time of changing public opinion, thought Jason. He'd often heard his grandfather, an Army veteran, mention all the protests in the U.S. around that time, and how discouraging the prevailing attitude was for returning soldiers.

Jason scrolled down to a picture accompanying the article. He zoomed in to a group of young Marines and a smiling Frank Wright. Jason sat back in his chair with a pleased expression just as Jake entered the room.

"Well don't you look like the cat who ate the canary! What's up?"

"Look here, sir. Recognize the writer's name?" Jason moved aside so Jake could get a full view of the computer screen.

"Is that who I think it is?" Jake bent closer to the screen and squinted. "Oh yes! I know that name. Martha Stanton. Good work, deputy."

"It's not much," said Jason, but he looked pleased. "Just a little connection."

"But who knows when a little connection might lead us to bigger connections?"

"Have you heard from Atkins yet, sir?" Jason took a quick screenshot of the article and sent it to the printer.

"No, he hasn't had much time with the body yet," said Jake, "but at the scene he told me he's sure it was a knife. Judging by the entry wound."

"Guess we'll have to wait for him to get back to us," said Jason. "I hope it's soon. Those guests at the mansion don't strike me as the types who will let us question them for long without demanding their lawyers."

"Demanding is right." Jake said. "What a group. And now we know there are some curious connections in that group. We need to get more information as fast as we can. The article you found is a start."

Jake grabbed his jacket off the hook. "Get your coat and let's go back out and check the crime scene again. Looks like the rain's let up for the moment. Maybe if we're lucky the wind has died down too." He shook the water off his jacket making a small puddle on the floor. "I want to see if we can recreate Frank's movements this morning. Who was the last person to see him alive inside the house?"

"And who met him on the trail by the creek?" Jason pulled his cap off the hook and followed his boss out the door.

"That's the million-dollar question, Dove," said Jake. He opened the door of the cruiser and slid inside.

***

The weary owners of the Compass Rose Bed & Breakfast sat in the kitchen watching as Emma chewed the top of her pen. A pitcher of iced tea and a pink-flowered ceramic platter holding a half dozen cinnamon rolls sat in the center of the table.

Nanette's work boots, caked with mud, stood by the back door on a small woven green and yellow rug. They leaned as though she'd kicked them off in a hurry and three dripping raincoats hung on the hooks next to the door. Marguerite's usually neat hair was ruffled, and Jane's apron was tied in a hasty knot rather than its customary neat bow. It was obvious that the ladies had gathered quickly to meet with Emma.

"You're gonna get ink all over your mouth," said Nanette as she leaned back in her chair. The wooden slats creaked as she pushed against the frame. "When I was in first grade, I bit the top off one of my pens. The teacher was mostly upset about me using a pen instead of a pencil. In fact, she said it served me right to have a mouthful of black ink."

"Well, maybe she was right," said Marguerite, winking at Jane.

"Humph," said Nanette.

"Cinnamon roll, Emma?" asked Jane, ever the hostess. She held up the platter.

Emma's heart twisted as she looked at the dear faces around the table. These ladies had worked so hard to get their bed & breakfast up and running. And now someone in the very first group of visitors had been murdered.

"Thanks, but not now. I know it's true that food always helps during times like these, right, Jane? I'd love to take one back to the library with me, though. Now let me go over these details to make sure I have everything down correctly." Emma cleared her throat. "So. Number one. You heard Sarah Davis ask her husband, Andy, if he 'did it'. We assume that she is speaking of the murder of Frank Wright, correct?"

"Yes, Andy was very angry and said, 'Now my own wife thinks I'm a murderer. 'And he pounded or kicked something in the room," said Jane. She grimaced. "I was worried about him hurting his wife. And I'll admit, I was also hoping he didn't damage any furniture."

"Number two. You heard Sarah ask Andy where he was at two this morning." Emma looked at Jane.

"Right," said Jane. "She said he wasn't in their room when she woke up." Jane folded and unfolded the paper napkin in her hand, scattering a few crumbs in the process.

"Do we know if Sarah told Jake that Andy was missing then?" asked Emma.

Nanette shook her head. "No. None of our crazy guests had much to say when Jake or Jason questioned them. They're all a piece of work, I'll tell you."

"How do you know what they said to Jake?" asked Marguerite.

"Well, sounds do carry in this house, and I might have been listening. A little," said Nanette with a guilty look. "And the fact that Sarah wasn't forthcoming with this information means she suspects her husband. I think this is enough reason to call Jake Preston in to arrest Andy Davis for murder."

"Come on, Nanette," said Marguerite. "Jake is going to need more than a few heated words between a husband and wife to charge someone with murder. We can't go accusing people without solid evidence." She poured more iced tea into each of their glasses.

"Well, Jake does need to send someone to stay here overnight with Terri," said Jane. "Or we all need to stay here with her. I can't stand thinking she'd be all by herself in a house with a possible murderer."

"That's true." Emma looked thoughtful. "I know. I'll volunteer to sleep over here until this is resolved. As long as the rooms have locks on them, that is. I can look around and listen while I'm here."

"The rooms all lock, yes," said Jane. "And that would be great, Emma, thank you! I'll let Terri know right away to fix up one of the two attic rooms for you. These were originally the servants' quarters, but we have fixed them up really nice. They each have their own bathroom. You'll be quite comfortable."

"Yes, thank you, dear," said Marguerite. "I'll admit I'm not too keen on sleeping here. I'm bushed."

Nanette nodded. "And I can't leave my animals on the farm, so this is a great idea, Emma."

Jane signed with relief. "I can't wait until this investigation is over and this group is gone. You know, my friends, it's going to take nerves of steel to keep moving along with this endeavor." She put her now-shredded napkin on the table and patted it.

Nanette said. "Well. Steele is my name, you know. And nerves of steel are my forte. We can do this. Don't want to be quitters, now, do we?"

Jane and Marguerite shrugged and smiled.

"That's the spirit, friends!" said Emma, as she pulled her phone out of her denim bag. I'll call Jake right now and see if he can come over and talk with us before I go back to the library." She paused. "And ladies. Let's not let him know right away about my plans to sleep over here. He'll find out soon enough."

The ladies looked at each other with raised eyebrows, then back at Emma. They nodded in unison.

***

Rain pounded on the cruiser roof as Jake pulled into the driveway and paused for a moment to take in the grandeur of the old house. "No matter how often I come here, I always marvel at this place. It's a true piece of craftsmanship."

Jason nodded in agreement. "Yes sir, I guess I started noticing the house just recently. I grew up around it and really hadn't paid much attention to it until now."

"Funny how we tend to glance right over things we see every day. Amazing and beautiful things that newcomers exclaim over. Like the mountains around here," said Jake. "Now let's make a run for it through this torrent."

The men threw up their hoods. They made a dash for the wide porch and rang the bell.

Emma opened the door with a surprised look. "Well look what the storm blew in! Your extra sensory perception must be working overtime today. We were about to call you. Come on in the kitchen and dry out. We have some things that might interest you."

"Well, good afternoon to you, too, Miss Kramer." Jake wiped his wet feet on the wool entry rug. "Why am I not surprised that you are here?"

"The ladies invited me. Like I said, we were getting ready to call you when you showed up on the doorstep like a couple of drowned rats."

Jake noticed the parlor was empty of guests. He half-expected to see folks lounging around the place sipping tea, playing cards, or doing whatever garden tour members do in their spare time on a stormy day.

"Welcome, gentlemen. Did Emma tell you we were about to call you?" Marguerite rose from the table and moved to the stove, turning on the burner under the kettle. "I'll heat some water for hot tea. Or maybe you'd prefer iced tea. And we have cinnamon rolls made fresh this morning."

Jason smiled and gave Jake a hopeful look.

"Please don't bother, Miss Marguerite." Jake motioned for Marguerite to sit back down

"Jason and I only came to take another look at the crime scene by the creek and speak to the guests again. We also need to take each of your statements."

"Really, Chief, you don't think one of us killed that man?" said Nanette. She shook her head and rolled her eyes at Jake.

"Standard procedure, ma'am," said Jason. He returned Nanette's severe glare with a smile. "And I wouldn't mind one of those rolls, if it's alright with you, Chief.They smell wonderful."

"Go ahead, Dove, dig in," said Jake.

Marguerite put a cinnamon roll on a plate and handed it to Jason. "Tea?"

"No tea for me, ma'am, but thanks anyway. We've been drinking gallons of coffee at the station."

"We need a statement from everyone on the premises," said Jake. "Whatever you three ladies can add will help us. And we need a statement from Terri, too.

"Let's just say so far, your guests haven't been very forthcoming in their statements."

"You can say that again," Nanette shook her head. "I think you ought to arrest Andy Davis right now."

"Oh? On what grounds?" Jake looked over at Jason.

"Slow down, Nanette. You're getting ahead of yourself," said Emma. She smiled at the older woman and flipped her notebook to the last page of her notes. "Jane heard a conversation between Andy and Sarah Davis at approximately 10:50 this morning in which Sarah asked her husband if he had killed Frank Wright."

"Maybe we'd better let Jane tell me what she heard," said Jake.

Jane shifted uncomfortably in her chair. It was obvious she didn't like center stage. A tenderhearted woman, she disliked sharing negative information about others. "Well, I was cleaning upstairs and freshening up the rooms when I overheard Sarah and Andy talking," Jane began. "I wasn't eavesdropping mind you, they were kind of loud…an argument really." She stopped to take a breath and Nanette jumped in.

"She heard Sarah ask her husband if he killed Frank Wright," said Nanette. "Now if his own wife suspects him, then I think you ought to arrest him immediately and get that murderer out of our house." She folded her arms, fully satisfied that the case was closed.

"Is that true, Jane, did you hear Sarah question Andy about Frank's murder?" asked Jake.

Jane nodded. "She wanted to know where he was in the middle of the night. He wasn't in their room around two o'clock."

"Well, that's interesting," said Jake. "We'll have to ask her about this. Of course, we need some hard evidence before we can arrest anyone. Can we use the library again to interview the guests?" asked Jake.

"Of course," said Marguerite. "We want to help any way we can."

"And don't forget, we'll be taking statements from each of you too. And Hiram. When Terri gets back, would you let her know as well?" Jake peered out the kitchen window and looked for the gardener. "Is Hiram working outside in this rainy weather?"

"Where is Hiram?" asked Jane.

"He's usually in the kitchen with you ladies when there's food," said Jason. "I can't imagine him missing these delicious rolls." He licked the icing off his fingers and put his plate in the sink.

"You're right. We haven't seen him since this morning when he was eating his oatmeal here at the kitchen table," replied Jane.

"Hard to say where he is right now," said Marguerite. "I think I heard his van, the Green Hornet, pull out of the drive early this morning. He sometimes likes to go fishing in the rain. Hiram makes his own schedule."

"Then was he here when we found the body?" asked Jake.

Marguerite and Jane looked at each other. "No, can't say he was here when we heard the news," said Marguerite. "He left the kitchen right around the time we called you."

The door from the dining room swung open and Andy Davis peered in. He pulled back in surprise when he saw Jake and Jason. "Oh, well. Sorry to bother you," he said. "But a couple of us were wondering when you planned to serve lunch. Since we're like prisoners here and we can't leave." He glared at Jake.

"Tell your group we'll serve lunch in the dining room about one o'clock," said Jane.

"Thanks, I'll let them know." As Andy closed the door, he added, "We're getting hungry."

"Terri's out getting groceries right now," Jane said.

"We'll go set up in the library," said Jake. "Would you let the guests know we're here to speak with them again, individually? We'll do our best to be done and out of here before their lunch is served."

"Certainly." Jane rose to call the guests. "They can sit in the parlor while they wait to talk to you."

"I can help you with lunch, Marguerite," said Emma. "I don't have story time at the library until three o'clock. I can stay a little longer. I'll give Cara a quick call and let her know. I'll sweeten the deal and promise to bring her one of your cinnamon rolls when I come back."

Jake cleared his throat, "Um…Emma, can I talk with you a minute?"

"Okay, sure," said Emma. She gave Jake a curious look. "Marguerite, I'll be right back.

"Take your time, dear." Marguerite smiled as the two walked outside.

***

Jake and Emma stepped out onto the wide porch. They were sheltered from the rain, but not the wind. It howled and moaned around the corner of the house. "So, what's up?" Emma asked.

Jake said. "I feel like a broken record. Every time something comes up, it seems like I'm warning you to be careful."

"You are a broken record," said Emma patting his arm. "Every single time. But you should know by now, Jake. I'm good at what I do."

"I know that, Emma. But being good at sorting out clues and coming to conclusions doesn't take away the danger factor."

"I believe I could have figured out that wisdom on my own," said Emma. "After all, I've been involved in the capture of two killers and had my life threatened twice. I know the risk. It's the same risk you face every single day."

"Yes, but that's what I get paid for." Jake sighed. "At least keep your phone with you, just in case you need to call me. And I'm sorry if I'm acting like a fussy old biddy. I only want..."

"...To make sure I'm safe. I understand, Jake," said Emma. "But these are my friends, and I want to make sure they're safe, the same way you want to make sure I'm safe. It's what friends do. And, besides, right now, you have an assigned officer here on the premises 24/7."

Jake leaned against a column on the wide front porch and glanced at the young officer who sat on the wicker settee several yards away. At least the wind would make it hard for him to overhear their private conversation. Jake had hoped to have a quiet talk with Emma, to let her know he thought of her as more than only a sleuthing buddy. This conversation wasn't going the direction he'd hoped. He felt like a patronizing uncle instead of a potential beau.

He lowered his voice. "I know your investigative skills are amazing, but you're not a trained police officer. Last fall, I had that experience on the mountain that nearly took my life. Facing one's mortality has a way of putting things into perspective."

"If life has taught me anything, it's that you can't live in fear of what could happen. Or dwell on the past," said Emma. Her voice softened. 'We've both experienced tragedies, Jake. Maribelle dying so young and leaving you to raise Kate by yourself, and my Eric taking all of our dreams with him when he died. Life isn't fair, but that doesn't mean we stop living...or stop trying to protect those we love. I'm not going to waste another minute of my life paralyzed by the fear of 'what if". These are my dearest friends, and I'm certainly going to be here to protect them anyway I can."

Jake reached out his hand and gently touched her cheek. "Just be careful Emma. We're dealing with a murderer here. Keep vigilant and stay safe...for me."

***

It was 2:30 by the time Jake and Jason returned to the police station. At least, no urgent calls had come through to take them away from their immediate task of finding a killer. They'd interviewed the B&B guests for a couple of hours, with no further breakthroughs. Sarah and Andy had been vague and unhelpful. Jake intended to find out what they were hiding.

"A busy day wouldn't you say, Jason?" Jake hung up his jacket for the second time that day. "I'm glad to be back in the office. My instincts are telling me we dig a little deeper into Andy Davis."

Jason slumped down into his chair. "His financial records might be of interest, especially when his wife said they put all their savings into this health franchise deal of Wright's."

"I hate to admit that Nanette was right, but at this point, Andy Davis looks like our main suspect." Jake sat on the top of one of the desks in the large open area. "He's definitely linked to Frank in this business. Money can be a powerful motivator."

"Let's see what else we can find out about Sarah's father, John Westmoreland. We know he was a former Marine colonel and is now a successful banker. How does he feel about his daughter and son-in-law mixed up in this franchise?"

"We still didn't get a decent answer about where Andy was at early this morning," said Jake.

"Getting some hot cocoa in the early morning with no one to corroborate his story, not even his wife. "Jason opened up his notebook.

"Yeah, and even she suspects him. But we need some hard evidence for motive, not just speculation."

Jake's cell phone buzzed. "This is Justice Atkins. Gotta take this, Dove. But let's see what we can come up with in the next hour." He pulled out his phone and hurried into the hallway, eager to hear something that would give them a break in the case.

"Hello, Justice. Preston here."

"Afternoon, Jake. I have some information for you on Frank Wright. Hold on to your hat." Atkins cleared his throat, and Jake could hear papers rustling on the other end of the line.

"He died from complications of the stab wound you saw, combined with some kind of poisoning. The stabbing alone would have been a serious injury if that was all that had happened. But he also had some kind of poison in his body. His blood showed significant acidosis, and his kidneys had begun to shut down. Must have had some pretty significant neurological deficits, too. Then the bleeding and trauma of the stab wound accelerated his death. My guess is ethylene glycol poisoning. Antifreeze. But I need to have that confirmed for you. We don't have a quick test for ethylene glycol. But his symptoms point to the kind of organ damage you see with that type of poisoning. Frank Wright was likely already dying of poison when he was stabbed with a sharp instrument like a knife. From the front, as you saw."

"So, you're saying the cause of death could be both stabbing and poison?"

"I'm saying we can't yet point to which of these things actually caused his death. Perhaps both."

"Wow, didn't expect that. Poor guy. What's the estimated time of death?" asked Jake. He sat down at his desk and reached for a lined tablet and pen.

"I'd say somewhere around four in the morning. He would have lingered a while until the effects of the stab wound did him in. But he would have been very sick from the poison, perhaps even unconscious."

"The county sent in a team to go over his room at the B&B and they've already worked the crime scene along the creek where I found his body. I need to get this information to them right away. Thanks, Justice."

"Sure. And I'll be back in touch as soon as I can confirm the poison in his body."

"Wow, who would've thought? Two separate causes of death." Jake shook his head. "Thanks, Justice. Call me the minute you have test results."

Was only one person responsible for Frank Wright's death? Or were two perpetrators working separately to do him in. Jake scribbled a quick list of details and tasks. First and foremost, he needed a warrant to search all the guest rooms at the Compass Rose right away. He had to move fast on this case while the clues were fresh and before someone else was hurt.

Thursday Evening

May 30

"Wait, what? You're getting married?" said Emma. She looked from Mia to her Uncle Albert. Inside his cage, Molasses meowed, but Emma didn't notice. "When? How?"

"We wanted to tell you, dear, but no time seemed to be just right," said Mia. "You stay so busy… Well, we've been busy too." She laughed and looked up at Albert.

"Sure have! We 've been trying to make our plans and get things in order," said Albert. "Come have a seat, my dear." He placed his hands on Emma's shoulders as he guided her into the living room toward the plump rose-colored sofa. Emma sank down among the mound of overstuffed pillows and placed the cat carrier on the floor.

"Things in order," Emma said. "You make it sound like you're planning a funeral."

"Quite the contrary, my dear, we are planning a life." Uncle Albert beamed with delight.

"Yes, and we're glad that you're here," said Mia. "We can finally share all of our plans with you." Mia and Albert stood together, their arms wrapped around each other. They looked at Emma expectantly.

Emma continued to stare at Mia, her father's younger sister, and at Uncle Albert, her mother's favorite uncle. A family affair, to be sure. She knew they'd been seeing a lot of each other. But...marriage? Molasses scratched at the cage and meowed more loudly.

"Let Molasses out, dear, while I go get us some cookies and tea," said Mia. "I think we could all use some refreshments, and then we'll tell you everything." Aunt Mia signaled to Albert to follow her. "Come help me in the kitchen, Albert, while Emma gets Molasses settled."

Emma shook her head in disbelief as she watched them walk arm in arm out of the room. She leaned over and snapped open the door of the cage. The cat jumped into her arms.

"What do you think about this, Molasses?" asked Emma. She rubbed the cat's soft fur while Molasses purred. This house had always been her safe haven, and Aunt Mia her confidante. It wasn't that she didn't love Uncle Albert too. She was happy they had found each other. But since her mother had died, Aunt Mia had always been the one Emma turned to—had always been there for her. Emma thought of her bedroom upstairs. The first room on the right with the bright yellow walls and four-poster bed. Emma had picked out the yellow and pink floral bedspread herself. It had always been her room, a shelter that surrounded Emma with warmth and love. But how would this marriage change things?

"No one makes cookies like your Aunt Maria," said Albert. Walking without his cane, he carefully carried a tray of cups, saucers, and a plate of chocolate chip cookies to the coffee table. "It must seem odd to you my dear, but as I told Jake, since this angel of a woman accepted my fumbling proposal, I've been besotted."

"Jake knows?" said Emma. She raised her eyebrows and shook her head.

It was at this moment that Aunt Mia walked into the room holding a teapot.

"Oh, Emma," said Mia. "Why the long face? We thought you'd be happy for us."

"I am happy." Emma said. "But I'm not so sure I like the fact that Jake knew your plans before you told me. My competitive streak, I guess." She smiled weakly. "It's just such a... surprise."

"It came up in our discussion about Kate," said Albert. "I'm not sure if I should say anything, but he has asked me to be named as Kate's guardian. Naturally, with such a big decision, I had to take him in my confidence about my upcoming marriage to Maria. It would affect us both if I became Kate's guardian." Albert looked to Emma for some sign of understanding.

"I did know Jake would be talking to you about Kate," said Emma, "but he never said anything to me about your marriage." Emma reached for the cup of tea her aunt had poured for her. The three sipped their tea together in silence.

"Well, to the young man's credit, I swore him to secrecy," said Albert. "I'm sure he'd have said something to you otherwise."

"Yes, we would never want you to hear this from anyone else but us," said Mia. She touched Emma's hand. "You are dear to us both. We want you to be a part of this, Emma, the marriage and our life after."

Emma bit into the soft goodness of a warm cookie. "So, when are you two planning to have the wedding?"

"Soon," said her aunt. "In fact, very soon. Two weeks to be exact."

Emma choked and put down her cookie. "Two weeks? I'll say that's soon. Can you get everything ready in such a short time?"

Mia smiled. "Well, we have had a few more weeks to think about it than you've had.

Emma rolled her eyes.

"We'll get married in the church," Mia continued, "and have the reception here at my house. Well, our house. Although, it will take some time to combine our households. Moving all of Albert's books over here will be quite an event. We'll definitely need more bookcases." Mia smiled at Albert and squeezed his hand.

"One more thing, Emma," said Mia. "I want you to be my maid of honor."

Emma's eyes widened. "Wow. In two weeks, you say?"

"I plan to ask Jake to be my best man," Albert said. "As the father of my great-granddaughter, he's family." He paused. "I hope he will accept."

"Does my dad know?" Emma asked. She couldn't stand thinking that she was the last to know.

"Yes," said Albert. "I felt it only proper that I ask your father for your aunt's hand in marriage. He gave us his blessing and agreed to give his sister away."

"We hope you will give your blessing, too," said Mia, hesitating. "Do you remember the conversation you and I had last year, Emma? I reminded you that we're not victims of our circumstances; that we always have choices. We can choose to make our lives different. Better."

Emma nodded. "Yes, I remember."

"I choose a life with Albert for as long as we have together. One full of companionship, love, and maybe even some adventure." Mia smiled.

"You know I love you both dearly, and I only wish you the best," Emma said. "I'll be honored to serve as you your maid of honor, Aunt Mia. Uncle Albert, I can't think of a better choice for your bride. And I hope life gives you many years of love and adventure." She rose to kiss her aunt's cheek and squeeze her uncle's hand.

***

Jason paused at the entrance to Jake's office. The door was open, but it didn't feel right to just barge right in. He knocked lightly on the door frame. "Sir?" he said. "Got a minute? I have a few things to show you. Found an interesting bit about Andy Davis. If you have a minute, I have it up on my computer."

"Sure, Dove," responded Jake. "What've you got? Jake followed Jason to the outer office.

"Well, looks like Andy's had several judgments against him in civil court cases in Northern Virginia. Failure to pay credit installments to a computer store, unpaid damages to rental property, defaulting on a car loan. From what I see here, he's in plenty of financial trouble. These cases are recent, two of them in the last few months."

Jake peered at the screen. "Print these reports out for me, Dove. I'd like to ask Mr. Davis a few more questions. In fact, let's bring him right now. I want to know more about the nature of his relationship with Frank Wright. And where he was at two o'clock this morning?"

"Shall I go pick him up?" Jason stood and reached for his cap.

"Yes," said Jake. "And we have two possible causes of death, Dove. Atkins said our victim had lethal poison in his system in addition to the stab wound. Possibly antifreeze poisoning.

Jason whistled through his teeth.

"But you go on now and get Davis in here," Jake continued. "I'll stay here and wait for the warrant to come through. As soon as it does, I want a team ready to search the Compass Rose."

***

The rain had left the fresh smell of moist earth and Jason inhaled deeply as he jogged up the steps of the mansion. "Good evening, Billings." He nodded at the duty officer on the front porch and headed to the kitchen. It smelled of sugar and blueberries and Jason could see two pies cooling on the counter. It looked like more were baking in the oven.

"Why, hello Jason," said Jane. "Please, come in. Can I offer you a piece of warm pie and a cup of coffee?"

"Thank you, ma'am. But I'm afraid this isn't a social call."

"I don't expect it is," said Jane.

"Do you have any idea where I can find Mr. Davis?" said Jason.

"I suppose he's in his room, top of the stairs, first door on the right. I haven't seen him since lunch. The Davises are in the Katherine Room."

"Thank you. If you'll excuse me, I'll go see if I can have a chat with them."

"Of course."

He took the steps two at a time and rapped sharply on the door of the Katherine Room. "Mr. Davis? This is Officer Jason Dove, Custer's Mill Town Police. Please come to the door, sir."

He heard footsteps shuffle toward the door.

Sarah Davis stood in the doorway, her eyes red and swollen, dark hair tousled. Her clothes were wrinkled and her feet bare. "He's not here, Officer," she said in a weary voice. "I don't know where he is. He left after lunch sometime."

"He left? But we have an officer at the front door. He didn't say anything about anyone leaving the premises. He'd have notified us if Mr. Davis left." Jason hoped that was true.

"Must've left through a less-obvious path, you know?" She sat down on the unmade bed.

"Well, may I look around your room, all the same, ma'am?" Jason gripped his cap in his hands. The boss would be angry.

"Sure, be my guest. But he's not here," said Sarah.

Jason looked under the bed, in the armoire and behind the heavy curtains. Nothing. He needed a word with Officer Billings.

When Jason returned to the kitchen, Billings stood by the counter, holding a plate with a piece of blueberry pie. His fork was poised, ready to place a large bite into his mouth. He froze when he saw Jason.

"Officer, what are you doing in here? You're assigned to stay on the front porch. Have you been on duty all day since you were told to report?" asked Jason. His voice was sharp.

The young man swallowed and set his plate on the counter before he answered. "Yes, sir. I've not left my post all day. Except to help Miss Terri carry in some groceries. And to sample this pie. Miss Jane said it's just out of the oven." He looked at Jane. "Isn't that right, Miss Jane?" He looked back at Jason.

"Oh, now, Jason. Officer Billings has been doing a fine job." said Jane." He helped me get down the flour and even kneaded some of the pie dough and rolled it out for me." Jane smiled at the pudgy young man. 'He's been quite a help to me today." She waved her hand toward the unfinished piece of pie. "Now finish that pie. You've earned it."

"Ma'am, Officer Billings had a job to do today, but it wasn't helping you make pies. We now have a suspect missing and this is going to complicate our investigation further." Jason looked at officer. "Did you see Andy Davis leave through the front door or through this kitchen today?"

"No, sir. I did not. Where did he go?"

"If I knew that, I wouldn't ask you. I'm going to look around the grounds. I expect to see you standing at attention at your post and acting professional while on duty. No more of this lounging around and pretending to be a pastry chef. Have I made myself clear? Chief Preston will be very unhappy and so am I." Jason didn't wait to hear the officer's reply.

Seething over the sloppy work of Billings, Jason searched the common areas of the house, including the pantry and all the large cupboards and closets, but Andy Davis was not in the building. Where would he go, without a car, and no bus service in this town? Would he just walk away?

Was he suicidal? Jason hoped not.

He walked quickly to his car through the rose garden. He punched in Jake's phone number. It only rang once before Jake picked up.

"Dove? Do you have him?"

"No sir. He's not here in the house, sir. No one has seen him since lunchtime. Including his wife. I'm going now to search the grounds for him."

There was silence on the phone and Jason squeezed his eyes shut.

"What was our officer doing? How could he let a potential suspect get out of the house?" Jake struggled to keep his voice at a level tone. "He was supposed to prevent this very thing."

"There are two doors in this house, sir, and the kitchen exit isn't visible from the front door," said Jason. "I found out Billings deserted his post a couple of times to help Mrs. Allman in the kitchen. I told him you'd be very unhappy. At least Davis doesn't have transportation. There's no bus service here. Hope he didn't call a taxi, though."

"Let's hope so, Dove. Let's hope so. I can't believe we let him slip by. Tell Billings he'll be relieved of his duties as soon as a replacement arrives. I'll call for one right now. And tell him I'll be filing a formal report on his behavior. Unacceptable. I'll also put out an alert for Davis. Maybe someone will pick him up. Stay there and find out what you can. Warrant should be here any minute. There's no time to waste. Gotta move fast."

"Yes, sir," said Jason, but Jake had already ended the call.

Jason walked back to the veranda to deliver the reprimand to a chastened Billings, then began to make his way around the manicured lawn and gardens.

He had just completed his search when the familiar rusty green van pulled into the driveway and circled around to the garden cottage. Jason remembered that old bucket of bolts from years ago, back when he was a young kid. His school friends used to sneak around and try to peek through the dusty windows, but Jason always stayed back out of view.

Hiram creeped him out. And the condition of that van. Did the corrosion around the wheels and the door handles make it look older than it really was? Come to think of it, Hiram probably looked a lot older than he really was as well. The long gray hair. The grimy baseball cap. Jason waited until Hiram had closed his vehicle door before he walked toward the older man.

"Catch anything?"

Hiram grunted and moved around to the side door and began to pull out his fishing gear.

"Stringer looks empty," Jason nodded toward the bare chain.

"Nothin' worth keeping," Hiram grunted. "Or if it was I gave it to feed the poor," he added as an afterthought.

"A lot of poor people hanging out around the river in a rainstorm, is it?" Jason peered around Hiram's scrawny form to look in the back of the van. It was still fully furnished with daily necessities even though Hiram no longer had to set up house in his vehicle. The garden cottage on the Brubaker estate was a world away from the way Hiram used to live, Jason thought.

"Our Lord fed the 5,000 with five loaves and two fishes," Hiram muttered.

"So he did," agreed Jason, "but I haven't seen too many multitudes living by the riverbanks around here."

"You want something in particular?" Hiram asked.

"Not sure," said Jason, as he surveyed the cottage and the neat beds of pinks and snapdragons. "See anything unusual around the place the last day or two?"

Hiram turned and walked toward the cottage as though he hadn't heard Jason's question.

"Hey, Mr. Steinbacher," Jason called, "I'm still talking to you."

Hiram turned. "The eyes of the Lord are upon every place. Beholding the good and the evil."

"Yeah, I figure so," said Jason. "But what about your eyes? Have you seen anything out of place lately? You know, something missing? Something not put back where it should be?"

Hiram shook his head. "The wicked plot against the righteous and gnash their teeth at them; but the Lord laughs at the wicked, for he knows their day is coming."

Jason sighed. Quoting the Holy Bible was okay. I mean, who was going to fault the man for speaking the word of God? But it did get frustrating when a man was trying to get some answers out of the fellow. "That makes a lot of sense," said Jason, his patience wearing thin, "but can you tell me what that means in everyday language? You know. Words I can understand."

Hiram closed his eyes as if trying to call back words he seldom used. "My shed out there." He pointed toward the old building in the back of the cottage.

"Yes?" Jason nodded encouragingly. "Your shed. What happened in your shed?"

"Creepers." Hiram scratched his grizzled chin, still unable to find the words he seemed to need.

"You mean somebody was creeping around your shed?" This interested Jason and immediately he wondered if this could be where Andy was hiding.

Hiram said. "More than once."

Jason pulled out his notebook. He restrained his excitement. The old guy was finally talking. He didn't want to mess it up or scare him away now.

"Let me get this down. You say several times you've noticed someone around your garden shed?" Jason scribbled some notes. Just enough so he could remember exactly what Hiram said.

"Late night. Rustling like rats."

"Did you happen to get a glimpse of anyone? Anyone you could describe?"

But Hiram was already walking away again. Jason knew that was all he would get from him this time around. Maybe Jake could get more information out of him. People talked to Jake.

His gaze went to the old garden shed. It looked like it could topple over if a strong wind came by. Whitewashed planks of wood framed the outside of the building. The sun had faded them so that the wood grain showed through. He guessed it must be pine since he could see the knots in the wood. No telling how old the thing could be or what was kept in there. Years of accumulating things he suspected, both Hiram's and the Brubakers'. No time like the present to take a look, thought Jason.

Worried the hinges would not hold, he opened the shed door a crack. Immediately, his nose was assaulted by the pungent odors of dirt, gasoline, and motor oil. He was wary as he lifted the flashlight from his belt and opened the door. The rusty hinges creaked and the door leaned to one side. The outside light pierced the dusty darkness. It took his eyes a few seconds to adjust as he stepped inside and looked around. His first impression was exactly what he expected—an old shed full of odds and ends. A wooden ladder was hung on the back wall. Jason suspected that it couldn't have been used for a long time since several rungs were missing. Ropes, assorted chains, and cords were tacked to the rafters on nails. At least there's some attempt at order, thought Jason. He walked around the room carefully, checking in corners and looking for places where someone could hide. A long workbench of sorts was against the wall to the left. It too leaned slightly. Jason moved closer to get a better look at the table and its contents.

A bag of potting soil, old work gloves, rusted hand spades and several seed catalogues were strewn across the top. A small pile of soil still looked moist and Jason surmised that Hiram used this old bench recently.

He stepped back and looked down under the table. A line of cans and bottles covered the space below. Not a place for someone to hide, but maybe there's something here that might interest the Chief. Jason took out his notepad and wrote down a few of the items: cans of paint, paint thinner, weed killer, turpentine, car oil, glass cleaner. And antifreeze.

Antifreeze. Jason felt a thrill of excitement. He couldn't wait to tell the chief.

"Find anything?"

Jason spun around, startled. Hiram was standing in the doorway, blocking the meager light.

"Not really," said Jason. "It doesn't appear that anyone has been hiding in here."

"Didn't say someone was hiding in my shed," snapped Hiram. "I said they was creeping around."

"Can you tell if anything has been disturbed?" Jason watched as Hiram moved around the room. It was obvious he was used to navigating through the obstacles of wheelbarrows, lawn mowers, and old cans.

"Can't say for sure. Just a feelin'," said Hiram. "I know someone's been here. Not certain what for."

Jason closed his book and took one last look around the room. He was eager to talk to the boss. His eyes fell on a woman's straw hat that sat on a peg behind the door. The silk roses around the brim were faded to a soft grey. A brown wicker basket hung next to the hat and inside were flowered print gardening gloves.

"Are these the ladies'...Miss Marguerite's or Miss Jane's?" asked Jason.

"No sir, they belonged to Miss Bertha." Hiram moved toward the door and held it open. "I like having them around. Never know when she might need them to go out in the garden to cut some of her roses."

"But she's ...." The old man was gone before Jason could finish his sentence. Of course, Hiram knew Bertha was dead. Strange man, thought Jason as he felt a chill run down his back. He pulled the shed door shut. Better get back to the Chief and give him my report. He knew Jake found Andy's disappearance disturbing. Jason's discovery in the shed could be the clue they were waiting for.

***

The dining room at the B&B was abuzz. The guests, seated around the table, awaited the evening meal. No one had seen Andy since lunch-time.

"No, for the hundredth time, I do not know where Andy has gone." Sarah sat surrounded by the rest of the members of the tour. She gave the group a defiant glare, but the effect was muted by her red-rimmed eyes and blotchy face.

"We don't mean to upset you, Sarah, but his absence does make him suspect." Isobel spread a generous slab of butter on her roll.

"Suspect for what? Murdering Frank? He's no more suspect than any of you." Sarah wiped an angry tear from her cheek.

"I do not appreciate being treated like a criminal," blustered Isobel. "Nor being held captive in this dreary house. We have rights, don't we? Can this Chief Preston really make us stay here if we don't want to?"

"Sister, it's a murder investigation. I think he has a right to keep us here. I'm sure everything will be settled very soon. After all, he's questioned us twice now. He should have all the information he needs."

"What I want to know, dear sister, is why we should be suspects? We didn't even know Frank Wright. You knew him didn't you, Martha?"

Martha looked at the old woman. She had sat in silence during the prattle, and squirmed now that the attention was directed to her. "Yes, a long time ago though. We hadn't kept in touch."

"From what I can tell he was a conceited, self-serving man who obviously schemed people out of their money. Isn't that right?" Isobel directed her final comments back to Sarah. "Did he take your money, young lady?"

"That's none of your business."

Marguerite, Jane and Terri were in the kitchen putting finishing touches on a meal for their irritated guests. They looked up at each other with raised eyebrows as they overheard the tense conversation through the dining room door.

Terri shook her head. "These people," she said with a sigh.

"I'm hoping a nice meal will help calm them down," said Jane. She mopped her damp brow with a paper towel.

"Yoo-hoo! Anybody home? I'm here to save the day." Nanette called through the back door where she was exchanging her work boots for a pair of nearly clean tennis shoes. "Need my indoor shoes to serve our honored guests, I suppose. Isn't the food ready yet?" She surveyed the cluttered counters and rolled up her sleeves. She looked around the room at her disheveled and somber friends. "What gives here, ladies? Looks like you all just swallowed lemons! Give me a job to do. No doubt the natives are getting restless."

"That's an understatement if I ever heard one. That poor child, Sarah. Why don't they leave her alone? It's obvious she didn't know where Andy was going," said Jane. Her phone gave a loud jangle and she stepped into a corner to answer it while the others continued to put the food on serving trays.

"I doubt they'll appreciate our efforts," said Nanette. "But, here, let me ladle that soup and you can deliver it."

"Well, let's hope those blueberry pies make up for the sparseness of the meal." Marguerite spooned salad dressing into small bowls.

Isobel pushed the door open and stood at the doorway of the kitchen, hands on her hips. "Oh, a sparse meal, is it? We are hungry. What kind of soup are you serving?" she said. She gave the pot a dour glance. "I don't want one of those ridiculous cold consommés like watermelon or cucumber or gazpacho or such."

"I assure you it is a regular, hot vegetable soup. One of our favorites," said Marguerite. She glanced at Terri with a look of amused irritation. " We're ready to bring out the soup, and we have plenty of rolls to replenish the bread baskets, too."

"I just spoke with Jake," said Jane, returning her phone to the countertop. "Officer Billings called him and said Andy was back on the premises. Jason is out by Hiram's shed, and Jake's on his way. Plus, he said he has a warrant to search the rooms of the guests. He's asked that we keep them in the dining room until he gets here."

Marguerite fanned her flushed face with her apron. "Oh, what else can go wrong with this day?"

"Does this mean he's getting close to an arrest?" asked Terri. "A warrant has to be issued by a judge."

"I think it means he has a strong reason to suspect someone in this house for Frank's murder," said Nanette. "Definitely something has developed in the case."

The doorbell rang. "That can't be Jake already," said Jane. "I just got off the phone with him.

"I'll get it," said Terri. "Would you all check to see if our guests need anything more right now?"

Terri opened the door to a damp and exhausted Andy Davis, accompanied by Jason Dove. Billings stood behind him. "He's supposed to stay right here until the chief arrives," Billings said, his eyes downcast.

"Well, Mr. Davis, we're certainly glad to see you." Terri moved aside to let Andy enter. "We're serving supper right now. I'll get you a salad while you go have a seat at the table with the others."

Terri gathered the ladies around her as they returned to the kitchen. "Andy…he's here…in the dining room. At least Jason's with him," she whispered, looking nervously toward the door.

"What should we do?" asked Jane.

"I say we feed them and keep them all in the dining room until Jake gets here," said Nanette. "Andy Davis won't try anything while Jason's here. At least I don't think so."

***

Jake grabbed the warrant and headed toward his car. His phone buzzed as he reached the cruiser. He pulled the door open with one hand and balanced his phone in the other as he slid into the seat. "Excellent, Dove! Glad you were still on the premises when Davis showed up. Keep them all there. I'm on my way right now." He turned on his flashing lights and sped toward Rosemary Street.

Jake's patrol car crunched along the mansion's gravel lane. A county van was parked on the circle next to the rose garden. Great, thought Jake. Forensics is here already. Things should move along quickly now.

Jake stopped to deliver a few stern words to the chastened Officer Billings before he entered the house. He hoped a replacement officer would arrive soon. There was no excuse for such sloppy work. It was a good thing for Billings that Davis had returned on his own.

The forensics team was waiting in the parlor when Jake entered the mansion. "You beat me here. Nice work. He nodded toward the closed dining room doors. "I'm sure they aren't too happy about being kept at the table, but I hope Dove and the intrepid ladies who run this place managed to hold everyone there."

"I think they can hold their own." The man smiled. "I'm Mike Peters, new team leader. Quick work on the warrant."

"Yeah, they came through for me. Just so you know, we don't have a murder weapon yet. I want that weapon found." Jake handed Peters the official papers.

The team spread out, while Jake joined Jason and the guests in the dining room. Nanette and Marguerite stood with their backs to the kitchen door. The expressions on their faces made him smile. Those two would have made great cops.

"Thanks, ladies. Jason," Jake said. "If you wouldn't mind staying where you are for a few moments longer, I'd appreciate it."

"Of course, Chief," Nanette said. "The Compass Rose guard contingent, at your service."

Marguerite nodded in agreement. "We'll be serving dessert in about ten minutes—fresh baked blueberry pies. Can I get you some?"

"Thanks, but we need to get to work here. Maybe you can wrap up a couple of pieces for Jason and me to have at the station tonight. I have a feeling we'll be working very late."

"Of course, glad to do it." Marguerite poked her head into the kitchen to ask Jane and Terri to set aside some pie for the hardworking town policemen. Then she resumed her erstwhile guard-duty position, standing tall and erect by the door.

"Well, folks," Jake gazed at each person seated around the table, "We're now officially searching all the rooms here and we have a warrant to do so."

Isobel and Martha rose.

"What? How dare you," said Isobel. "You can't do that. My things are my business and no one else's."

"I'm afraid they're police business now," said Jake. "And please sit down everyone. You are all to remain in this room with us until the forensics team has finished their work."

Isobel continued to mutter. She advanced toward Jake as he backed up to block the exit to the hall. He stood at the doorway, legs spread apart and hands on his hips. It was clear to Isobel that he was not going to budge. She returned to her seat and glared at him, then at her sister.

"What did I do?" asked Glenda. Her cheeks were flushed and perspiration stood out on her forehead and nose.

"Oh, hush up, Glenda," snapped her sister. "Just let me concentrate. I can't believe they think they can rifle through our belongings like that." She drummed her fingers on the wooden arm of her straight-backed chair.

Sarah Davis appeared unaffected by Jake's announcement. Andy's behavior had left her emotionally spent. She sat in her chair, her bare feet skimming the floor like a child, her gaze focused downward. Tears trickled down her face and splashed onto her jeans. She dabbed at them now and then with the cloth napkin in her lap.

Andy was the only guest not seated at the table. He stood apart from the group and refused to meet anyone's eyes. He held his fists clenched at his side.

"Mr. Davis. Please step out here." Jake pointed to the doorway and stood aside for Andy to come through. "Now then, Mr. Davis. You left the premises today after you were told to remain. We'd like to ask you a few questions down at the station. Officer Dove will escort you back there now." Jake motioned for Jason to join them.

"I don't have to tell you anything unless you're charging me with a crime. And I won't go with your officer without an attorney," said Andy.

"Well, sir, it's true you don't have to talk to us. We're not arresting you. Yet. And you're welcome to have an attorney present. Do you have someone in mind? Surely you can understand we find it troubling that you left the mansion without a word to anyone. This is your opportunity to explain your reasons to us."

A shadow crossed Andy's face. "Fine, I'll go with you. But I don't have to answer you. I'm not guilty of anything." He glanced back through the doorway at Sarah, then looked away when he saw her tear-stained face. "I'm not, Sarah. I'm not a killer," he muttered.

"Mr. Davis? This way, please." Jason motioned for Andy to walk out of the mansion in front of him, and the footsteps of the two men faded away as they headed out the front door.

***

Mike Peters came to the doorway of the dining room and motioned for Jake to come closer. "Sir, may I have a word?"

"Yes, but do me a favor, first, won't you? I had to send Dove back to the station with Davis. Would you get Billings from the porch and tell him I need him to come in here for a few minutes?"

"Sure, be back in a few seconds."

He returned with Billings who assumed Jake's position in the doorway as Jake stepped into the parlor and out of sight of the guests.

He motioned to Peters. "Let's go into the library, Peters," he said, his voice low. "This place echoes like nobody's business." Jake knew all ears in the dining room were straining to hear what they were saying.

Jake closed the heavy double doors behind them as they stepped into the library. It smelled of old books and polished wood. "What do you have for me, Peters?"

Peters held out a gray metal strongbox about the size of a mailbox. It was secured with a large hasp and padlock. "Found this in the William Room. Where those two sisters are staying, I believe."

Jake shook the box gently. It was heavy, and items inside clattered around. "I'll ask the sisters if they're willing to unlock this for us. If not, I'll have to get another warrant to take it down to the station and open it. They won't like it, that's for sure. Thanks, Peters. Keep looking. Sure would like to find the murder weapon soon."

Jake carried the box back to the dining room with gloved hands. Isobel rose in alarm when she saw what he held. "Give me that right now!" she shouted. "I'll have my lawyer ruin you if you hold on to it one more minute." She walked closer to Jake. Isobel was a tall woman and stood almost eye to eye with the Custer's Mill police chief.

"Ma'am. We have a lawful warrant to search these premises, and this item was found here in the house." Jake forced his voice to take a neutral tone. "Will you open it for me, so I don't have to get another warrant to take it to the station and cut off the lock?"

"What? Cut the lock off? Don't you dare." Isobel locked eyes with Jake.

"Ma'am. I'd advise you to control yourself and avoid getting yourself into trouble. Sit down. Now. I insist." And he took a half-step closer to Isobel so that her nose almost touched his face.

Her voice shook with anger and she seemed on the verge of tears. She gritted her teeth as she spoke. "I will not, repeat, not, give you the key. You have no right. You have no right to take our private things…". Her voice trailed off as she continued to meet Jake's steady gaze.

After several tense moments, she turned on her heel and stomped back to her chair.

Glenda grabbed Isobel's arm and said, "But, sister, you have to give him the key. Don't let him cut the lock. You know it's the one Father gave us back in 1950. Please, don't do this."

Isobel pushed Glenda's hand away. She sat in stony silence.

Jake felt a small twinge of guilt at her distress, but he felt a thrill of excitement about learning what secrets the box might hold. In truth, he was unsure if he could really get another warrant to take it away, but he hoped the threat would work in his favor.

Isobel's head jerked up. "Alright, I'll give you the key. But I am strongly protesting your actions, and I will talk to my attorney tomorrow." Isobel's words were tinged with a stronger German accent than usual. "I need to go to our room to fetch the key." She stood and brushed past Jake with disdain.

"Go with her, Peters, please," said Jake as Isobel headed into the hallway. "Keep an eye on her while she's in the room."

Isobel whirled around and glared at Jake. "You will hear from my attorney very soon, Mr. Police Chief. Yes, you will." And she marched up the stairs followed by Peters, who studiously avoided looking back at Jake.

***

Isobel thrust a brass key into Jake's hand, her lips set in a thin line. "Well, Officer. Go on. Get it over with."

The box sat on the large table in the center of the library. Jake looked at the key in his hand, then returned it to Isobel. "Ma'am, why don't you open it?"

Her look of surprise was short-lived, but satisfying to Jake. He preferred to have a separate warrant that allowed him to open the box himself. By letting Isobel open it, he'd save himself the headache of possible legal action. He just hoped she'd go for it.

Isobel stared at him for a long minute.

"Fine," she said. She turned the small, ornate key in the oversized padlock, removed it with care, and flicked open the hasp. "There, Officer. You got what you wanted." She slipped the key into the pocket of her skirt, and stood back with her arms crossed over her blue cotton blouse.

"May I take a look at the contents?" Jake asked.

"Well, isn't that the whole idea?" replied Isobel. "Silly question."

One by one, Jake took out the contents of the box. First, he lifted out a small wooden container filled with old coins. Valuable old coins, if he wasn't mistaken. He set it on the library table and pulled out some silver flatware, two teaspoons and three forks. He looked up at Isobel.

Next, he saw a bag made of soft, purple cloth. Inside he found three pearl necklaces, a man's ring set with an emerald, and several sets of gold and silver earrings set with pearls and semi-precious stones. "My mother's and my father's jewelry and our own coin collection," Isobel said, her face defiant.

Jake pulled out a string of sparkling stones that looked like diamonds, bundled by itself in the strongbox. He dangled it from his hand before he set it on the table with the other items. A white envelope contained a Purple Heart decoration and accompanying paperwork. Interesting, he thought.

Isobel offered no further explanations, but sat with lips pursed, silent and seething.

The bottom of the box was covered with old letters and newspaper clippings. One by one, Jake unfolded them and arranged them in a single layer on the table. He pulled out his phone to snap photos of all the items. He made sure he'd captured all the writing on the letters and articles. He knew there'd be no second chance at this box.

The box was now empty, and still there was no sign of a murder weapon, or anything that would link the box and the sisters to Frank Wright's murder. Jake sighed, and Isobel smiled. "So, officer, nothing here to interest you after all. You have invaded my privacy for no good reason. As I said, I will be calling my attorney tomorrow and you will be hearing more about this unnecessary action. And now, may I return my things to the box?"

"Yes, ma'am, you may."

"And I will take the box away with me, back to the dining room where I can keep it in my sight."

"Yes, ma'am, that will be fine." Jake wondered how soon he'd be called up to answer for his actions on the box. Just what he needed, in the midst of a murder investigation that was not going very well.

He watched Isobel slowly replace each item with loving care. She closed the hasp, and secured the padlock. Tucking the box under her arm she walked back into the dining room.

Her sister half rose in her chair as she entered the room. "Did you get everything back?"

"Of course I did," said Isobel. "And I told that overbearing police chief he'd be hearing from our attorney. The nerve of that man!"

"Oh, I wasn't worried," said Glenda. "You always know what to do."

Thursday Night

May 30

"Have a seat there, Mr. Davis." Jason nodded toward a worn metal chair with a stiff green upholstered seat. He gathered up papers and folders from his desk and cleared out a spot in the middle to put his notebook. "Can I get you some water?"

"No," said Andy. "Just get on with it."

"Okay, then," said Jason, as he sat down at the desk. He desperately wanted to do a great job with this task. He knew the boss would come back soon. Jason imagined being praised for asking all the right questions and getting a stubborn man to answer as fully as possible. He cleared his throat.

"Why don't we start by you telling me why you left the mansion today, and where you went?"

"I was exploring the house." Andy's tone was flippant. "It was very boring, you know, sitting around, practically under house arrest, nothing going on. Anyway, nobody was in the kitchen when I wandered in there.

That fat officer was helping someone carry in groceries at the time, so I just slipped out. I went for a long walk. Then I came back. End of story."

He sat back in the chair and looked pleased with himself.

Jason tapped his pencil on his notebook. "Where'd you go? We searched the grounds, and didn't see you. And it's been a very rainy day."

"Took that little footbridge across the creek, then followed the creek until it met up with a river. Think it's called the North Fork River, maybe. Climbed up under a rock ledge out of the rain and sat there quite a while. It was kind of cold. I made a sort of pillow with old leaves and took a little nap. Actually, I didn't mean to be gone so long, but I was pretty tired and slept."

"Okay, let me ask you something else. Somebody heard your wife mention that you were not in your room last night around two in the morning. Where were you?"

"She told you that?"

"No sir, but it was overheard. You were arguing, I understand."

"You mean those old biddies were spying on us, listening to our private conversations? Man, am I going to give that B&B a bad rating."

"Where were you at 2 a.m., Mr. Davis? You seem to go missing rather often."

"Well, I couldn't sleep, so I decided to go down to the kitchen and find something to eat. Or drink. Really wanted another glass of wine. Or something stronger."

"And then?" asked Jason.

"And then, I returned to my room. They only had sweet iced tea and lemonade to drink. Not the kind of stuff that helps you zone out."

"Okay, now tell me about your relationship with the deceased, Frank Wright."

Andy looked disgusted. "He was a weasel. He tricked my wife and me into investing in his pyramid scheme to sell health foods. He ruined us, financially. We used all our savings and then some to buy in. Then we learned about all the hidden costs, and how we hardly earn anything for the first year. I found him repugnant, but I didn't kill him. Can't say I'm sorry he'd dead though. Frank Wright was a real deadbeat, pardon the pun." He folded his arms across his chest.

"Okay. You admit you hated him, but wouldn't harm him, that right?" said Jason.

"Yeah, that's right. You don't have anything on me except that I took a little walk today. But that's not murder."

"I understand you've had several judgements against you recently, unpaid bills, collectors."

"What about it?"

"Strong reason to want to do someone in for causing your troubles."

"No, it's not. It's a reason to despise someone, but not proof that I would touch a hair on his big ugly head," said Andy.

"According to my research, your wife's father was a U.S. Marine officer in Vietnam, is that correct? Did he know Frank Wright?"

"I don't know who he knew then or who he knows now. Of course, my wife thinks he knows everything, like a male Mary Poppins, her daddy. Practically perfect in every way. And I'm done answering your questions. You want to ask more questions, you're gonna have to arrest me. You have no proof I have anything to do with Frank Wright's murder. You know it, and I know it. So, take me back to that glorious mansion now, Officer. I insist."

"Fine, let's go," Jason snapped his notebook shut and the two men stood up. He restrained his irritation and disappointment that his questioning hadn't brought any new information to light. He drove Andy Davis back to the house in silence.

***

"Would you look at that? "Mike Peters said. He gave a low whistle as his latex-covered fingers pulled aside an ornately patterned silk scarf.

A fixed-blade knife in a sturdy brown leather sheath lay at the bottom of Martha's lower dresser drawer.

"Better get the police chief," said his assistant. "He'll want to see this before we bag it."

"Say what?" Jake stuck his head in the door. "I was passing by when I heard my name. Do you need to see me?"

"You need to see this!" said Peters, holding the tip of the sheath in his gloved hand. "I'm not totally sure, but I think this is a Randall attack knife. Our military used them in Vietnam."

"We most definitely need to get this beauty to the lab," said Jake, as he peered closely at the knife. "This could be the break we've been waiting for."

Peters nodded. "Hope so, Preston."

"You take care of sending that off. I need talk to Miss Stanton," said Jake. "She has more explaining to do."

The disgruntled guests sat in silence around the dining room table. All eyes turned toward the door as Jake entered the dining room, and he stared at each one in turn.

"Who do you want to cross-examine first?" asked Isobel, as she drew her cardigan around her thin shoulders. "Since you're intent on blaming someone, whether or not you have good reason."

Jake smiled at her, but didn't answer. Instead, he turned toward Martha. "Miss Stanton, I need to speak to you. Come this way." He motioned toward the door.

"What? Wait a minute. You can't take me away like that."

"Miss Stanton," said Jake, his patience thinning with each word, "I'm not taking you away. I want to ask you a few questions, and I think it might be better if we talk at the police station."

"You're arresting me, then? On what charges? I want my lawyer. I won't say a word without my lawyer.

"Please. Calm down, Miss Stanton." said Jake. "Nobody is arresting you. Of course, you may have a lawyer present if you wish, but I hardly think it necessary at this stage."

"I know how the police work. They sweet-talk you into thinking they're simply throwing out some routine questions. And then, bam! You're accused of a crime, found guilty, and hanged. All in a day's work for the lawman."

"Miss Stanton, I don't know where you get your ideas about policemen, but I assure you, that's not how we operate. I simply want to talk to you about something we found in your room. I'm sure there's a reasonable explanation for it."

"What? What did you find? You can talk to me here. I don't want to leave this house with you!"

Jake lowered his voice. "We found a knife in your room, Miss Stanton. A Randall attack knife, to be specific. Like those the military issued during the Vietnam War."

To his surprise, Martha threw back her head and laughed. "A knife," she choked, "an army knife? And you think I killed Frank with an army knife? Now that's rich."

Jake waited for Martha's hysterical cackle to calm down before he spoke. "We don't know that this was the knife that killed Frank, but we would like to know what it was doing in your room. The owners of this B&B told me that Frank had mentioned his knife was missing."

"Okay, okay. I'll go down to the station with you. I think this is all a set up. Something planned by that surly youth, Andy. I get the impression he'd do anything to take the suspicion off himself. Including planting evidence in my room."

Jake opened the cruiser door for Martha and latched it behind her.

It was less than a mile to the police station, but Jake could feel Martha's angry gaze on the back of his head the whole way there.

***

"Here's your coffee. Sugar?"

Martha shook her head.

Jake sat down at his desk. He was so weary. He hoped he could think clearly enough to ask the important questions in this interview. "So, Miss Stanton. I understand you knew the victim while you were a correspondent during the Vietnam conflict," he said.

"He has a name, you know. The victim. Yes, I knew Frank back then. I was a naive kid and he was...." Martha's voice trailed off.

"And he was what?"

"Goofy, energetic, full of himself. He never saw a stranger. He'd often carry on long, one-sided conversations with the Vietnamese soldiers. Of course they didn't have the slightest clue what he was saying, but that didn't stop Frank."

"Were you two ever...," Jake paused as he searched for the right words, "...ever romantically involved?"

"Ah, romance. What an interesting word." Martha set her cup down on the edge of Jake's desk. "The word romance implies that there are two people involved. But in our case, I believe I was the only one who ever saw anything romantic in our situation."

"You mean you had feelings for Frank that he didn't necessarily reciprocate?"

"You can say it, Chief Preston. It's OK. I'm over it now. You can say that Frank used me for a good time. A few rollicking nights on the town with no strings attached."

"And how did that make you feel? The fact that he didn't take your relationship seriously?"

"If you mean did it make me kill him forty years later...no. "Martha looked past Jake to the darkness outside. She seemed lost in thought. "Back then though, who knows? If I had the means and the opportunity I might have pulled a trigger on him. It might have felt like motive enough at the time. He never told me he had a fiancé waiting for him back home."

"But what about now," persisted Jake. "Are you sure you haven't been harboring that anger for the past four decades? Letting it stew and boil under the surface? Are you sure that anger didn't finally get the best of you? Are you telling me the truth? Did you kill Frank Wright?"

"That's a lot of questions, Mr. Police Chief, said Martha. "I can save time and answer one final 'no' that covers everything. I did not harbor a lethal hatred for Frank, and I did not kill him. Now, if you are determined to keep me here and continue to pepper me with questions, I must insist on having a lawyer present.

"But you do know that we found a knife—Frank's knife—in your room. And you are aware that Frank was stabbed. Can you see where we're coming from?"

Martha thumped her fist down on the desk, threatening to topple the cup she'd set there. "Yes" she said, "I *do* see where you're coming from, and I can certainly see where you're headed. I told you already. Someone planted that knife in my room."

Jake gave her a questioning glance.

"Don't go all good cop on me. Why the polite questions? You think I killed Frank and you're waiting for me to say the wrong line so you can cuff me." She stood up and began to pace the floor. "Just say it. You already have me tried, convicted, and waiting to be hanged. Let's get on with it. Any further discussion on this topic will have to go through my attorney. I'm calling her tonight.

***

As Emma steered her car toward Rosemary Street she replayed the conversation about her aunt and uncle's upcoming marriage. She had expected to make a quick stop at Aunt Mia's house to drop off Molasses so she could spend a few nights at the mansion. Just until they found Frank Wright's murderer.

But now she found herself in the middle of wedding plans. She wondered what Marguerite, Nanette, and Jane would have to say. She was heading to the B&B now, but doubted the ladies would still be there. It was well past 9:00 pm.

Terri seemed grateful that she'd had volunteered to stay with her during the night. She was a tough lady, but had been spooked by the weird noises she'd heard. Footsteps, doors opening and closing. Not that Emma felt particularly brave herself, but she was intrigued by mystery.

She pulled her car into the driveway and parked next to the stone wall. She noticed a small light on in the foyer and lights on in the rooms over the porch. Everyone should be settled in their rooms by now. At least she hoped they were. Emma didn't want to engage in conversation with any of the tour guests. Definitely not a friendly or sociable bunch today.

She greeted the new duty officer, a young woman, on the porch. Before she could ring the bell, the front door opened and Terri stepped outside, drying her hands on a blue-flowered apron.

"Thank you so much for coming over." She hugged Emma. "Come on in. I feel pretty uneasy by myself with this group of oddities, especially since we don't know if one of them is the killer."

"I agree. You shouldn't be in this house alone with these folks. It's no problem really." Emma carried her small suitcase into the front hall. "I hope everyone is settled for the night."

"Pretty much," said Terri. "They had tea in the parlor this evening, and they've all gone to their rooms. I've finished cleaning up the dishes and checked the back door. Here, let me lock the front door, then I'll take you up to your room."

"I wish we had a second bedroom downstairs," said Terri, "but with all the rooms occupied on the second floor, the only space available is in the servants' quarters in the attic."

Emma shook off a sudden stab of uneasiness. "That will be fine, but how will I hear you if you need me?"

"You've got your phone, right? I can always call." Terri rounded the landing on the second floor and started up a flight of stairs at the end of the hall. Light shone from under the doors of the rooms. "I know this is a little out of the way, but at least you'll be comfortable. I dusted and aired out one of the rooms today. Put fresh linens on the bed and towels in the small bathroom. Marguerite insisted I place flowers in your room."

Terri opened the door at the top of the attic stairs. The dark void beyond made Emma cringe until Terri flipped on a light, revealing a short hallway.

To the right, Emma could see into a long room with slanted ceilings on both sides. Although the room was in deep shadows, she could make out furniture neatly stacked in the back half of the room—tables of all sizes, chairs of all shapes, and a massive fainting couch in the middle of the floor. "Wow, look at all this stuff. This attic is full of antiques."

"The Brubakers stored all of their discarded furniture up here after they no longer employed servants," Terri explained. "The ladies have taken some of the items downstairs to use, but as you can see there's still a lot up here. Here we are. This is the room you'll use." Terri opened a door on the left of the hallway and turned on a ceramic lamp just inside the room.

Emma's first impression was the small size of the room. She guessed the Brubaker servants didn't spend much time up here, so little space was needed. The second was an uncomfortable awareness of how remote the attic was to the rest of the house. A tiny dormer window was centered in the wall opposite the door, and a bathroom was tucked under the steeply pitched ceiling. She'd have to remember to watch her head in there.

"I never met Miss Bertha," said Terri, "but I feel like I know her. Aunt Jane and the others are so concerned with doing things the way Bertha would have wanted. They talk about all these belongings as though Bertha still owned them. You'd think Bertha was still alive."

Emma noticed the queasiness in her stomach once again.

"The room's okay, isn't it?' Terri looked at her friend with concern.

"Yes, of course." Emma smiled. "I'll be fine."

"Would you like some tea or hot chocolate? We also have some pie left if you'd like a snack."

"No, I think I'll read a little before bed," said Emma. "You don't need to wait on me, Terri. I'm here to help you, remember?"

"Yes, and I can't tell you how comforting it is to know you're here. Thanks again." Terri gave her friend another hug. "I'll go now and let you settle in. See you in the morning. The coffee will be on before 6:30. The ladies will be cooking by the time you get up. Good night."

"Good night," said Emma as she closed the door and turned the lock. She gazed around the cozy little room and noticed for the first time that the walls had been whitewashed. It gave the small space a lighter feel. A double bed covered with a flower-patterned quilt was tucked under the slanted roofline. A small lamp sat on a nightstand. A dresser on the side wall held another lamp and a bouquet of peach-colored roses in a crystal vase. "Of course, Rosemary Harkness–Bertha's favorite." Emma spoke aloud and leaned down to inhale the sweet aroma.

As she unpacked her few things, her mind went to Bertha and the Brubaker family. All gone now, but Billy. Poor Billy, he was trying to get his life together with his new business, but his past foolishness had cost him dearly—his family home for one thing. "What must it be like to have strangers in your home now, Miss Bertha?" Emma said. She froze as she heard a sound. A creak. Maybe it was Terri returning. She opened the door. Light spilled out of the room onto the slats of old oak flooring. Emma looked around but there was no one there.

She changed into her nightgown and managed to get ready for bed without hitting her head on the ceiling. She climbed under the covers, plumped up the pillows behind her, and picked up her book from the nightstand.

She was getting back into the story, when the creak came again. Emma listened. The smell of roses suddenly intensified.

Friday Morning

May 31

The sun was just beginning to rise as Serafina stopped her car in a small patch of gravel off the dirt lane to Bessie's cabin. After the heavy rains of the previous day, she was afraid to park in the grass. Getting stuck this far up the mountain would be a bigger adventure than she was up for today. This was her first solo visit back to the place since Bessie had died. Of course she'd been with that garden group the other day, but that had hardly counted as a relaxing trip. Those women were like free range hens, running all over the yard breaking off stalks of herbs to rub between their fingers. And then there was that poor man. Frank.

Serafina hadn't particularly liked him, He was too loud and pretended to know everything about the wild herbs she had shown them. But she hadn't known he would die the next day. She might have been a bit nicer to him. Maybe.

She had made the mistake of telling Nanette that she was coming up to look for angelica stalks. Nanette had almost insisted that she be allowed to come along to hunt for wild asparagus. That woman was as stubborn as a mule. Serafina had finally convinced her that she was only going for a quick trip and that she'd take Nanette up another day. It wasn't that she didn't like the older woman's company. In fact, Nanette was one of the few people Serafina felt understood her. If Nanette was going to judge your actions, she'd judge them to your face, not talk about you behind your back. That kind of straightforwardness was a rarity.

But today Serafina needed to be alone. Needed to inhale the mountain air. To listen to the quietness of Jenkins Hollow below.

The grass was still damp with dew as she spread a blanket under the ancient oak tree. She took her sketch pad out of her tote bag and opened the case that held her graphite drawing pencils. She couldn't remember when she'd last taken the time to sketch. The lines she drew were heavy and awkward at first, but gradually, her hand and her mind relaxed and she began to lighten her grip.

She sketched the cabin and the little building out back that held Bessie's distillery. Her moonshine shack as Petey Blue had called it. As far as Serafina knew, Bessie had never made alcohol in her life. She used the distillery setup to extract oils from herbs and flowers—oils she used for healing, relaxation, and for her Appalachian magic.

As a rule, Serafina didn't spend too much time ruminating and reflecting. She tried to live in the moment and to keep her memories in the past where they belonged. There was one point in her life that she couldn't seem to forget though. The years she spent in the gypsy camp in Romania. In rare quiet moments her mind always returned to that far away land. The makeshift shacks, the open fires, the vibrant colors. And the music. Oh, the music. She could hear the haunting violin melody now. *Voliv tut ages Voliv tut tehara Voliv tut mai but Desar mai anglal.* I love you today, I'll love you tomorrow, I'll love you much more than ever before.

A bee landed on her sketch pad. A hornet. She flipped the page up and tried to shoo it away, but it stuck tightly to the paper. Bumblebees and honey bees she could deal with. Hornets were creatures of another class. They were aggressive little monsters whose sting was worse than regular bees and unlike other bees, they could sting multiple times. She carefully laid her sketch pad on the ground and walked to her car. She felt silly running from a creature so small, but she'd rather be safe than sorry.

She looked up at Bessie's house. Quiet. Dignified, despite its shabbiness. Petey Blue was the only surviving relative that she knew of. She wondered what he would do with the place. There was no predicting Petey Blue's actions. He was a free bird. She hoped he'd keep it though. It would break her heart if some developer bought the land and subdivided it. A sudden breeze swept in from the south and she saw a curtain flutter. Bessie's ghost? She wouldn't be surprised. The old woman had an uncommonly strong spirit. Most likely she was still watching over her place from some dimension, some realm.

The wind picked up even more and a dark cloud crept up the valley below. They were probably in for a passing thunderstorm. She'd turned to pick up her sketchbook when she heard it. The violin. The song. *Voliv tut ages Voliv tut tehara.* Oh great. She really was losing it. That's what happens when you let yourself get lost in memories. She should know better. A spattering of rain mixed with her tears as she went to retrieve her sketch pad. I'll love you tomorrow, I'll love you much more than ever before.

***

Emma woke with a start. For a minute she didn't know where she was. A beam of pale light flickered underneath her door. She gave her mind a minute to focus, and then remembered she was at the B&B.

Her sleep had been fitful, with dreams full of creaky floors and doors opening and closing. She reached for her phone on the side table. Six a.m. Something had woken her. She lay still and listened. Her ears picked up muffled voices. Slowly Emma pulled back the covers on the bed, and stepped cautiously to the door. She opened it a crack so she could see into the dark attic room and hear the hushed voices a little more clearly.

"Sister, I'm not sure we're going to find anything else up here. It won't be long until others start to stir." Glenda slid a drawer back into an oak dresser.

"Just keep looking," Isobel's whisper was a hiss. "This Bertha Brubaker was rich. No telling what treasures she left up here." She was peeking into a tall armoire.

"Here, Sister, see what I found in this purse? A brooch!" Glenda's voice rose slightly and she held up the ornate jewelry. "These could be sapphires. Now I know you're upset that Chief Preston looked through our box, but he didn't find anything that he was looking for. Our belongings are safe and now we can add to our treasures."

"Shh! Be quiet. We'll see how much that brooch will fetch for us. We need money. We'll have to sell a few things." Isobel continued going through the pockets of old coats. "We'd never have thought to come up here if we hadn't seen that girl, Terri, coming out of the attic door with some old linens. It was good luck for us she leaves it unlocked."

Emma could only see the backs of the two women but she could hear their whispered conversation clearly. They were up to no good. Should she confront the women now or wait until they left? She stood still watching.

"Glenda, look at this." Isobel stepped back from the armoire holding a long cane. "I believe this is real gold." Her voice was quiet but excited as she turned around, holding the cane out for her sister to see. "It'll fetch a pretty penny I think."

"Stop!" Emma stepped into the attic. "Give me those things. They're not yours." She approached the sisters and grabbed the cane out of Isobel's hand.

Glenda put her hand behind her back and both sisters stared at Emma.

"I'll take the brooch too," said Emma. Glenda reluctantly relinquished the ornate jewelry.

"Who are you?" asked Isobel. "We didn't know anyone was up here."

"I guess not," replied Emma. "Or you would have done your thieving at another time."

"We weren't going to take anything. We were just snooping a little," said Glenda meekly.

"At this hour? I don't think so. Both of you get out of here and don't try this again. You have no business prying around up here, or anywhere else in this house. Do you understand?"

Isobel and Glenda nodded and made their exit, heading down the stairs.

Emma watched as they left. She stood looking at the brooch she held in one hand and at the cane in the other. Definitely not your normal guests, she thought.

She dressed quickly and hurried downstairs to share this new development with the ladies. Jake would need to know too.

Emma could smell coffee and bacon as she approached the kitchen. She carried with her the brooch and the cane. No guests were downstairs yet, probably too early. She didn't expect to see the two sisters, either. If they had any sense, they'd stay in their rooms, out of the way.

"Good morning," said Emma as she opened the door and entered the fragrant kitchen. Marguerite and Jane leaned against the counter, coffee mugs in hand. Two large egg and bacon casseroles sat on the top of the stove ready to pop into the oven. Nanette and Terri were busy folding napkins. All eyes turned to Emma.

"How did you…? What in the world do you have there?" asked Jane.

"I caught those two old sisters rummaging through the dressers and wardrobes in the attic. They found these and were going to keep them." She held out the items and Marguerite took them. "Terri, I suspect these ladies have something to do with the noises you've been hearing. They tried to pass it off as snooping around, but they were planning to steal whatever they could."

"They probably took those spoons and other utensils we're missing," said Nanette. "Good thing Jake got that warrant to search their rooms yesterday."

"Terri, you didn't tell me Jake came with a warrant," said Emma. "Did he find anything? Or did he keep it all hush-hush?"

"I was so tired when you arrived last evening, I didn't think to tell you. Jake returned with a forensics team and went through all the bedrooms," said Terri. "We had to keep the guests all together. It was awful. They did seem excited about something they found in Martha's room. And old Isobel had a fit when Jake asked to go through her precious strongbox."

"Yeah, first Jason took Andy into the station for questioning, and then Jake took Martha in, too," said Nanette. "That Andy was AWOL for several hours."

"They brought them both back here, though," said Jane. "No arrests."

"Wow, lots of drama. Have you noticed anything missing?" asked Emma. She felt a thrill of excitement at the prospect of gathering more clues. Excitement combined with a bit of competition. She wanted to find out something Jake didn't already know.

"I plan to count all of our silverware," said Nanette. "It's solid silver, you know, not just silver-plated. I'm sure some is missing. After the hullabaloo last night, those old biddies have some gall trying to steal Bertha's treasures the very next morning."

"I'll stop by and see Jake first thing this morning," said Emma. "He needs to know what they've been up to. And, dear friends...please let me know if there's anything else I can do for you. Don't get discouraged by this terrible event. It has nothing at all to do with any of you or your lovely B&B. I'll volunteer to work with Terri on a fantastic new marketing campaign to drum up business. We'll get through this. Together."

"Hear, hear," said Nanette, as Marguerite and Jane raised their cups in salute. Emma hugged each one in turn before she headed out to report her findings to Jake.

***

He had caught a glimpse of Serafina through her car window as she pulled away from Jenkins Hollow early this morning. A dark silhouette behind tinted glass. But he didn't need to see any more. His heart lurched. He had to see her; to talk to her; to make her understand what really happened back in Romania. He would go to her shop. Hiram would take him. The old man was weird, but he could still be reasoned with. David leaned against the rickety porch post and looked out over the valley. How much more beautiful the world would be with Serafina by his side again.

He hoped it wasn't too late. But Serafina was a fiery one. She might not understand why he had to leave. He knew it was a mistake not contacting her, but he couldn't risk it. He could have put her life in danger too. And that was something he could never live with. He glanced around the kitchen in the old farmhouse. Even the wood burning stove and ancient pots and pans were more than he was used to in the caravan. It was funny what little you needed to survive. But the beautiful Serafina shouldn't have to live without modern conveniences. Who did he think he was? What could he offer her? Truthfully, he couldn't even give her a place as good as this rickety shack.

***

Jake arrived early at the police station. He was exhausted from the events of the day before. Three times they were at the B&B yesterday with little to show for it. He hoped to hear Atkins' confirmation that Martha's knife killed Frank Wright. Maybe then this case would start to fall into place. He walked across the hall to the kitchenette and scrubbed out his stained coffee mug.

Jake was on his fourth cup of coffee when he heard the front door open. He hoped it was Nanette bringing Kate by to see him. He felt like the worst dad in the history of humankind. He hadn't seen Kate for any length of time since Frank's body had been discovered. Most of the time she was at school or with a sitter. He preferred her to stay with Nanette, but the ladies were busy now taking care of the B&B. This investigation was sucking his life away. He needed a breakthrough and he needed it soon.

"Yoohoo! Anybody home?"

He knew that voice. Serafina Wimsey. Great, just like the devil to tempt me in my weak moments.

"In my office," said Jake wearily.

Serafina flounced in the door, turquoise rings flashing, flaming hair swirling, mischievous mouth twitching with amusement.

"Well don't you look like death warmed over! What's up, Mr. Jake-the-Cop?"

Jake said. "Look, Serafina, it's been a long couple of days. Sorry if my sunny self is not coming through. What can I do for you?"

"Sorry," she said, folding her long skirt behind her and sitting down in the metal chair by his desk. "Believe it or not, my visit is business. Could even possibly be related to your case although I don't see how."

"Go on," said Jake, his interest growing.

"Very early this morning I spent some time at Bessie's house. You know, just thinking. Tried to sketch a bit, but alas, that muse seems to be on vacation. Anyway, there were some strange happenings going on there."

"Such as?" Jake moved forward in his chair, all attention on Serafina.

"Well, I'm afraid it will sound stupid once I say it out loud." Serafina laughed ruefully. "But here goes." She pushed a lock of ginger hair behind her shoulder. "I heard a violin song. It was a tune I heard a long time ago in another time and another place." She smiled. "See, that sounds weird!"

"Tell me more," said Jake.

"There's not much more to tell other than I heard a fine violin playing an old gypsy song I used to know. I also felt like someone was watching me. That might have been Bessie's ghost, but the song I heard was real."

"And you think that song might be connected to the case somehow?"

"Probably not. And now that I'm saying this out loud, I'm pretty sure there's no connection. The more I talk the stranger this sounds." She rose to leave.

"Not as strange as you might think, Serafina," said Jake. "With a murder investigation, we look into every single clue— every unusual happening no matter how small. I'll send Jason out on a drive to Bessie's house later. Thanks for stopping by."

"The pleasure is all mine," she murmured. And this time Jake smiled.

***

Jake sat back down at his desk and stared at his notes. What was he missing? Andy Davis was hiding something behind his belligerence. But Jake had no reason to arrest him—not enough evidence. As far as he could tell Andy's only transgression was to make a bad investment with Frank. He wasn't sure he believed Andy's story about the time he spent in the woods to clear his head and make some sense of what was happening.

And Martha Stanton. She said she didn't know how the knife got into the drawer in her room. She did confess that she had given Frank the knife a long time ago, but she swore he had the knife, not her. Martha said how surprised she was that he kept it all these years. A memento, she said, from their time together in Vietnam. Jake had to let her go, too. He wasn't sure she had told him the truth but without evidence, little could be done.

"Jake, are you here?" He heard Emma's voice in the hallway.

"Back in my office. What are you doing out and about so early?"

"Oh, I wanted to see you before you got busy this morning. I stayed the night at the B&B."She wore a long white gauzy skirt with a pink flowered cotton top. And she'd taken extra care to arrange her dark hair in a loose bun before she got out of her car, in hopes that Jake would be at his desk. She was rewarded with his look of approval when she stopped in the doorway of his office.

"Terri mentioned something when I was there last evening before you came. She said you're her guardian angel. Just be sure you guard yourself, too." Jake motioned for Emma to step inside the office. He noticed a light scent of jasmine trailing into the office with her. It was pleasant.

"Have a seat." Jake pointed to the chair facing his desk.

"Thank you. Well, Terri shouldn't be in that house alone, and I was right. This morning I caught those two old ladies up in the attic going through Bertha's things. They were in the process of stealing a brooch and a gold-topped cane. If I hadn't stopped them, who knows what else they would have found and taken for themselves."

"That would be the Fischer sisters." said Jake. "We have reason to believe that they have been in trouble before for petty theft. Harmless... but they tend to take things that don't belong to them. Do the ladies want to press charges?"

"No, because I caught them in the act, they didn't get a chance to actually take anything. Maybe we need to keep a better eye on them. Too many valuables in the house to tempt their sticky fingers," said Emma.

The phone on Jake's desk rang. Justice Atkins' name flashed in the caller ID.

"Emma, I'm sorry but I've got to take this. Can you see yourself out? I'll check in with you and the ladies later this morning." He reached for the phone. "Justice, can you hold one minute?"

"I'm going," said Emma, standing up. "Just be sure you talk to Terri and Nanette. They may have more to share about these sisters." Emma walked down the hall toward the door. She admitted to herself she was irritated at Jake's quick dismissal. But she knew he was busy. Choosing not to dwell on it, she squared her shoulders and jogged down the outside steps, holding her skirt up to avoid tripping on it.

"Okay, Justice, what do you have for me?" Jake listened as the medical examiner gave his report on the knife found in Martha's drawer.

"Unfortunately, this is not your murder weapon...at least, not the knife used to stab Mr. Wright."

Jake pursed his lips in frustration. "So, it's not the murder weapon... hmmm. Can you tell me anything about the knife we found?"

"I would say it dates back to the 60's." said Atkins.

"As old as that? Well, I guess it would have to be that old if it was from the Vietnam War."

"Do you have an idea of how it came to be in the mansion? Forensics brought the knife to me and said it was found in a drawer in one of the guest rooms."

"Yes, Martha did say she had given it to Frank. At least that part checks out. Whose fingerprints did you find?" asked Jake.

"Two sets of prints were still on the knife. Prints of the victim and of one other person." Atkins paused. "I'll check Martha Stanton's prints against the second set."

"Your findings are interesting, but it doesn't get me any closer to discovering who killed Frank. Let me know if you find anything else and if you get a fingerprint match. I appreciate your quick work on this, Justice." Jake ended the call.

Jason appeared at Jake's door. "Did I see Emma leaving?"

"Yes, she had a run in with Glenda and Isobel this morning. They were snooping around in the attic."

"Did they take anything?" asked Jason.

"They tried, but Emma interrupted their heist. By the way, Justice Atkins just called and the knife we found wasn't the murder weapon. I feel we keep starting back at square one with this case," said Jake.

The scanner on Jake's bookcase blared. It was Mill County dispatch. "Rescue 50, respond to a 10-30 involving multiple vehicles on I-81, near mile marker 254."

"Grab your gear, we've got to go." Jake jumped up and took his gun out of his drawer. Both men headed to the front door. "I hope there aren't any fatalities in this pileup and we can get back here pronto.

Friday Midday

May 31

Jake and Jason were bone-weary when they returned to the police station after the interstate accident. It had been a miracle of sorts that the pileup involving six vehicles produced only three injuries, all non life-threatening.

Jake was grateful for that. But long hours were taking their toll on his thinking. He needed rest, but there was no time. He couldn't hold the guests at the mansion any longer, and they'd be leaving tomorrow morning, whether or not he'd made any arrests. At this point, there wasn't enough evidence to arrest anyone.

The spicy scent of oregano wafted from the paper bag that held their lunch subs. Jake almost felt guilty taking time to eat. The clock was ticking on solving Frank Wright's murder.

He sat back in his chair and rubbed his face with his hands. "We still have no murder weapon, so I've asked forensics to send a team back to the drag the creek again. It has to be somewhere. Atkins said the Army knife Martha had was too broad of a blade. The entry wound didn't fit. The weapon used on Wright has to be long and thin. I want it found. Today."

Jason nodded and headed to the little kitchenette. Discouragement showed on his face. The case was not moving ahead.

Jake rolled his chair close to his computer and began to print out two enlarged copies of each photo he'd taken last night in the library.

The printer was humming when Jason returned with two mugs of coffee and offered one to Jake. "Here you go, sir."

"Ah, thanks, Dove. That's the ticket. Maybe this will help clear some of the cobwebs out of my poor tired old brain. Now sit down over at that table, and let's look through this stack of photos I took. "He handed a set of printouts to Jason.

Jason moved aside several stacks of paperwork to make a space in the center of the small work table. There was silence in the office as the two men studied each photo. Jason spread several pictures at a time across the cramped space, and Jake flipped through his stack one at a time.

"Okay," said Jake. "There are several pictures of documents and newspaper clippings. It will take time to review each, but this jewelry... the pearls and the emerald ring, plus a lot of expensive-looking earrings... they're a place to start. Those women don't look the type to wear this kind of jewelry. I want you to check them out on the database and also look up any thefts of items like these. We need to know if our little old ladies are thieves, or if these items really did belong to their parents."

Jason looked intently at the photo of the coins. "And the coins, too, sir? I can check out stolen antique coins as well."

"Yes, do that. And then there's this flatware. Sort of unusual items to keep in a strongbox, wouldn't you say? I'm going to call the ladies and ask them if any of these items may have gone missing at the mansion."

Slow steps outside the office made the two men look up from their work. Professor Albert Nelson peered around the doorway.

"Excuse me, gentlemen, I see you're hard at work. Would it be too much trouble to talk to you for five minutes, Chief Preston?"

Jake sighed quietly as he stood to greet his guest. "Certainly, Professor, please come in. If you'd excuse us for a few minutes, Dove? Take the photos to the conference room and see what you can come up with."

Jason nodded. "Of course, sir." He gathered up the papers and his mug of coffee and left the office. Another interruption was the last thing they needed right now he thought, as he trudged down the hallway.

***

The professor cocked his head as he entered the office, raised his eyebrows and looked at Jake across black-rimmed eyeglasses that had slid low down on his nose. The severe look this gave the professor's face made Jake feel like he was back in the principal's office in elementary school. But the professor's kindly smile dispelled that unexpected old memory. He shook Jake's hand warmly and pushed the errant glasses back into place.

"Now Jake," said the professor, "I know you're in the middle of a big murder investigation, but I thought perhaps it would ease your mind to know that Maria and I have decided to agree to your request to be named as guardians for your sweet Kate."

"That's wonderful! Thank you so much, Albert," said Jake as he sat back down at his desk. "That's a huge relief. One less problem to worry about, for sure."

"Not that we'll ever need to be, mind you," he added. "You'll be around a lot longer than we will, but if it helps you to know...just in case...our answer is 'yes'."

"Please tell Mia I'm deeply grateful," said Jake. "I'll have Paul Stewart update my will and leave a copy with you. Now would you like to sit down for a moment? And can I get you some coffee? Or tea, maybe?"

"No, no. I'll let you get back to work, and I'm off to visit my sweetheart. We cherish every moment we have together. It's quite a blessing, you know, the company of a good woman. It's time for you to consider that yourself."

Before Jake could think of an appropriate response, the professor gave him a small wave and disappeared down the hallway.

Indeed, thought Jake. Perhaps it is time to consider that.

***

"Why, Mia, how are you?" Jane embraced her friend as she entered the hallway of the B&B. "It's been a while since we've seen you."

"I know, life can get busy can't it?" Mia unwound her scarf and draped it across a peg on a wooden coat rack in the entryway. "I can't believe what you three have done with this place. Not that Bertha didn't have a lovely home, but you have somehow drawn out the natural character of the place," Mia said. "I know I'm stumbling over my words, but you know what I mean."

Jane smiled. "We're having a crisis right now, as you know. But this place keeps us hopping. Always plenty to do, something that needs repair. How about a cup of tea?" she offered. "We're just cleaning up the breakfast dishes. Come on in. Sit and visit with us a while.

"I would like that. I know you have guests and now this terrible ordeal to deal with, so I don't want to take up much of your time, but I do have a bit of good news I want to share with all of you." said Mia.

"Wonderful! We could use some cheering up. Nanette and Marguerite are in the kitchen. You'll have us all in one place."

"This is such a pleasant surprise, Mia," said Marguerite as Mia and Jane entered through the dining room doorway. "How long has it been since we've just sat and talked?"

"Too long," remarked Nanette. "How about some coffee cake?" Nanette pointed to a plate holding freshly baked apple coffee cake left over from the breakfast. Without waiting for an answer, she sliced her friend a piece. "Here you go. We're getting pretty good at this baking thing. Andes Bakery better watch out."

Mia laughed. "Thank you! It looks delicious. I'm sure running a B&B is a lot of hard work, but as I was saying to Jane, you've done a great job of making Bertha's home feel cheery and welcoming."

"Yeah, well that's what we thought, but having a murder among our first guests is not the start we were hoping for." Nanette frowned.

"Now, Nanette, Mia doesn't want to hear about our troubles," said Marguerite.

"Well, Emma's already shared a little about your troubles, especially her concern for Terri staying by herself at night with your guests. That's why she decided to sleep here for a few nights. I'm cat-sitting Molasses while she's here."

Marguerite returned the kettle to the stove. "Yes, we're grateful Emma volunteered to come. In fact, only this morning she confronted two of our guests that were snooping around in the attic."

"Oh, my, whatever were they looking for?" asked Mia.

"Stuff to steal." Nanette snapped. "We think they stole some silverware. I plan to count it in a few minutes."

"Now, we don't know for sure," said Jane. "Emma said she'd stop at the police station and talk with Jake before she headed to work."

Mia looked with concern at her friends. "I'm so sorry for your troubles. Jake is a good police officer. I do hope, though, that Emma doesn't get herself involved too much. You know how she loves to play detective. Has since she was a little girl."

"So, you have some good news?" asked Marguerite. "We could use some."

Yes, some wonderful news, amazing news." Mia beamed. "Here, I've come to give you this." Mia reached into her purse and pulled out envelopes and handed one to each of the ladies. "Open them. I hope you will be as pleased as I am."

Jane was the first to speak. "This is great news! Congratulations!"

Nanette reached over and hugged Mia.

Marguerite got up to come around the table and give her friend a quick squeeze. "Very exciting, yes. But how? When?"

"Well, it all started when I went with Albert to Richmond when we were researching the library...you remember. We talked and talked. I always knew he was brilliant, a scholar, but I never knew he was such an interesting...and funny...man. We found ourselves enjoying each other's company. One thing led to another and we started seeing each other.

"Dating you mean?" asked Nanette.

Mia blushed, "Okay, dating. We've been friends for decades, but we never really took the time to get to know each other. You know. Our likes, our dreams. I have to tell you, after all these years of living alone, having someone to share my life with has been a wonderful prospect. I don't mean my family hasn't been supportive and always there for me, but this is different. This is special."

Jane read the invitation in her hand. "So, the wedding is in two weeks...at the church. Wow, that's soon."

"Yes, and we want you all to come back to my house for the reception. It will be a small gathering. I have such a small family, and Albert has only Jake and Kate."

Nanette, Jane, and Marguerite looked at each other and with a nod, they said in unison. "We'll have the reception here."

"Oh, no, I couldn't ask that of you," said Mia, "especially with all the trouble you're having right now. It would be too much of an imposition."

"Well, Miss Maria Kramer soon to be Mrs. Albert Nelson, if you think you and Albert can get married and this whole town not turn out, you are seriously mistaken," said Nanette. "Why, it's the biggest event since… well, since the university's marching band performed in our town parade back in 2005. That brought quite a crowd, remember?"

The ladies gave Nanette a quizzical look.

"We want to do this, Mia," added Jane. "It will be our wedding present for you and Albert."

"Yes, and we also have the most beautiful gardens at your disposal for fresh flowers for the church." said Marguerite. "Bertha's roses are in full bloom, just waiting for a special event to show them off."

"The church will look lovely with sprays of the peachy pink roses surrounded by baby's breath." replied Jane. "We can place them on the ends of each pew with bows of peach lace…oh, it will look stunning."

Mia took a sip of her now-lukewarm tea and smiled. "It is a blessing to have such wonderful friends. I'm so happy, I feel like I might burst!"

Friday Afternoon

May 31

"Hi Chief! Didn't expect to see you again so soon!" Marguerite held the front door open as Jake stepped into the spacious entry hall. A delicious smell of herbs and vegetables was in the air, and his stomach growled, even though he'd eaten a sub at the station only a couple of hours ago. It seemed like weeks since he'd had a home-cooked meal and sat down at the table with his little daughter.

"Marguerite. Ladies," Jake nodded to the group gathering in front of the grand staircase. Nanette, Jane and Terri were all there. Good, thought Jake. I can ask my questions to everyone at the same time and get back to the station. Time was ticking away and he felt the strain at the back of his neck that always flared up when he was stressed. Maribelle could always massage it away. For a second, he wondered if Emma knew how to massage tired muscles. He brushed the thought aside.

"Ladies, I need to ask you a few more questions, if we could sit down in the parlor for a moment. And where are your esteemed guests right now?"

"In their rooms, thank God," said Nanette with disdain. "Pondering their sins, I hope." She gestured toward the parlor. "Lead the way, sir."

After everyone had settled into their seats, Jake pulled out his notebook, and his phone for quick reference. He looked around the room. "So. Have any of you noticed any silverware or other items missing here at the mansion? I mean things are not just misplaced? Or anything else that struck you as odd."

"I have," declared Nanette. "We're missing that necklace off the St. Fiacre statue in the garden. Not worth a lot, but it was a fun decoration."

"I need exact details of anything that's missing. What did the necklace look like?"

"The necklace was nothing but rhinestones, but it was a long string," said Jane. They looked really pretty when the sun shone on them." She leaned forward. "And, Terri, didn't you mention to me that Isobel argued with Hiram about that leather satchel she carried? You thought it was strange."

"That's right, said Terri. "I'd forgotten about that. It did make me wonder what that irascible lady kept in the bag that made her overly protective of it."

Jake scribbled notes as the ladies talked.

"Well, Chief, I also took it upon myself to recount our silver sets, because I just had a bad feeling about those nosy ladies," said Nanette. "At least two teaspoons, two dinner forks, and I think maybe a knife and a dessert fork or two have disappeared.

"Now, Nanette, you have to double-check to make sure those last items weren't put away in the wrong place," said Jane. She looked at Jake. "We store the silver in two separate boxes in the dining room. Bertha was quite the entertainer. We inherited lots of flatware and dishes."

"I told you we needed to watch those two!" Nanette looked triumphant.

"What was the name of the silver pattern, Nanette?" said Jake. "Do you know?"

"One set of 16 place settings was engraved with a stylized "B" on the handles. That must have been the Brubakers' first set. Then there's also a set of 16 place settings of Francis I silver by Reed and Barton. Very collectible, I understand. Using the term "collectible" loosely in this case." She cleared her throat.

"Thanks, these are all helpful pieces of information. Anything else you've noticed amiss, ladies?" He visualized the photos he and Jason had started to review earlier. Without giving anything away, he needed to know if any of the strongbox items would be mentioned by the ladies. Certainly, a string of rhinestones was in their box. Some articles, like the jewelry, could be heirlooms as the Fischer sisters said they were, but he had his doubts. "Well, I value your perceptiveness. Anything you may have noticed will be helpful."

The ladies all smiled, pleased at the compliment.

Marguerite spoke first. "You know, the evening before poor Mr. Wright was killed, we attempted a social time of wine and snacks after dinner? It came out in the rather unpleasant conversation at the gathering that Mr. Wright's knife was missing from his room, and Miss Stanton said her Cross-pen set had disappeared, too. I believe they both thought it was those sisters who took their belongings."

Jake consulted his notes and flipped back a few pages. "A Cross pen set, you say?"

"That's right," said Marguerite.

"Hmmm. Interesting. Forensics listed a Cross pen set in their notes as having been found. But they found it in Miss Stanton's room. That warrants another questioning session with Miss Stanton, I believe."

Nanette looked at Jake intently. "Chief, something else is gone, I think. I was looking for the fillet knife in one of the kitchen drawers this afternoon, because I wanted to use it to prepare tonight's meal. I can't find it and I looked everywhere I could think of." Her eyes widened. "Oh my God. Do you think that could be the knife that killed Mr. Wright? From our own kitchen?"

"Now, ladies." Jake spoke quickly to allay the look of fear reflected on each face. "We haven't found the murder weapon. Let's not jump to conclusions. Forensics is dragging the creek right now to see if they can find any further clues to the murder. I'll be sure to let you know if they find anything that looks like a fillet knife. But right now, I have to get back to the station."

He stood to leave and the ladies accompanied him to the door. He paused and turned to look at the circle of worried faces. "Hold tight, ladies. Make sure to call Jason or me right away if you think of anything else that might have a bearing on this case, or if you see anything unusual at all."

He walked down the porch steps to a chorus of "yes, sir" and "absolutely, Chief."

***

Jason hoped the day would stay sunny. It had rained a lot lately, and he could see a few clouds had started to gather into dark grey clusters.

The road he drove along was enclosed by trees, sometimes opening up into a grassy field with grazing cattle. Jason felt vulnerable today — open to the mercy of what might be lurking at the forest's edge. Even the trees seemed menacing. Warning him to stay away.

He had no idea what to expect at Bessie's house. Serafina's description of "faint violin music, whistles, and an eerie feeling" were vague— not much to go on. Jason had never understood much of what Serafina said. Sure, she was pretty enough, but definitely not his type. Her winks and casual hugs made him uncomfortable. And most of the time he could make neither heads nor tails of what she said. Chief seemed to be enchanted with her though. He was of the opinion that Chief would be better off with someone sensible and normal, like Emma Kramer. And it was pretty obvious she liked him.

Jason shook his head. There's no accounting for taste.

He pulled up to the little frame house and parked at the bottom of the stone steps leading up to the front door. He took a deep breath, and ran up to the small porch. He knocked on the door and waited. Nothing. Only sounds were the creaking boards under his feet and the wind in the trees. Strange that not even a bird could be heard in all the forest around him.

With an involuntary shiver, he walked back down the steps and around to the back of the house. A small cleared area served as a patio of sorts. The ground was covered with smooth pieces of shale. Dozens of old flower pots, some with growing plants in them, and some with dead stalks sticking out were stacked around the edge of the stones. Bessie's own plant laboratory, he guessed.

He stepped up on the cinder blocks that served as the back steps to the house, and knocked on the wooden door that opened into Bessie's old kitchen. The door had once been painted white, but was now a splintered, weathered gray. He tried to peer into the kitchen, but the windows were covered with curtains, and he could only glimpse a bit of a wooden shelf lined with Bessie's jars and potions.

He called out, "Police. Anyone here?" A dark cloud scudded overhead, and put the surrounding forest into a sudden, premature dusk. "Police! Come out!"

A scrabbling sound in the undergrowth near the clearing made Jason jump down off the steps and crouch behind the steps, his weapon poised and ready. "Come out now! Who's there?"

A dark-haired, disheveled man stepped out from behind a stand of cedar trees, and stood, his hands raised above his head. "Don't shoot me, sir, please."

Jason stood up, his gun still pointed at the man. "Who are you and what are you doing here?" he demanded. His voice was strong, but his heart thumped in his chest and his hands were shook. He'd almost let off a shot into the trees. Thank God he hadn't done that.

"My name is David, sir. David Nicolescu. I have permission of Mr. Pete Blue to stay here in his old grandmother's house. You can ask him."

His foreign accent was strong, but Jason wasn't able to identify it. "I will most certainly do that. But I would like you to come with me to the police station as we have some questions we need to ask you."

"Are you arresting me, then?"

"No, my boss, the police chief, would like to talk to you, that's all. We're investigating a murder in our town, and maybe you know information that would help us. And I'd like to see your identification, a driver's license or something like that."

"I don't have such a document, sir, and you'll likely be wanting to turn me over to the immigration authorities. I hoped to avoid such a fate."

"We don't have to do that, and we won't do that. You come along with me to answer some questions, and I'll bring you back here when we're done. "Jason returned his service revolver to its holster. "You can put your hands down now, but keep them where I can see them. Just stay right in front of me."

"Is your police station near to the herb shop of a Miss Serafina?" asked David.

"It is."

"Then I shall find my own way back here after we are done. I have an important visit to make in the town."

"Very well, that's fine by me." Jason motioned for the man to lead the way around the house, and followed behind him. The man's head drooped, dejected. So, here was the source of Serafina's eerie experiences at this house. A real, live, undocumented human being, not a wood spirit or a supernatural being. Jason relaxed and felt cheerful at the positive outcome of his assignment. The Chief would be happy.

Jason opened the cruiser door for his passenger, and they headed back down the rutted mountain road toward the Custer's Mill police station.

***

Hiram leaned against the end of a sturdy wooden shelf filled with bags of teas and herbs. Although he'd never tell Serafina, he loved the exotic fragrances that permeated her Serendipity Herb and Tea Shop. The contents of each bag were identified with a neat hand-written label and tied with a bright bow of red, green, gold or blue, making the shelves look like a decorated Christmas tree.

Serafina stood in front of the counter packing more herbs into bags and carefully labeling each one as she finished. She brushed her exuberant red-gold curls out of her eyes as she worked. Filled bags and strands of ribbon lay across the end of the counter, awaiting the final touches before she put each bag on its shelf.

The two friends were comfortable in each other's presence, and long silences between them were typical. Hiram Steinbacher was not a man not known for his conversational prowess. Neither had spoken for the past ten minutes.

When Hiram cleared his throat and spoke in a solemn tone, breaking the silence, Serafina looked up with interest.

"The Lord will bring to light the hidden things."

"Yes, indeed, Hiram." Serafina shook the bag in her hands and placed it on the scales. "Perfect. I'm almost always spot-on with my weights before I weigh the bags. It's a little game I like to play. And, as you say, I'm sure the Lord would bring to light any errors I make if my customers ever feel shorted." She made a wry face.

"Judge nothing before its time." Hiram followed his response with an uncharacteristic laugh.

Before Serafina could ask him why he laughed, the heavy door of the shop creaked open, jingling the bells at the top of the frame. Both Serafina and Hiram stared at the visitor who peered around the door as if to ask permission to enter.

Hiram nodded and motioned for the visitor to come in.

Serafina's face paled and her mouth dropped. "David." A hoarse whisper was all she could manage. "It was you at Bessie's."

"Yes, my love. It was all I could do not to run to you when I first saw you there. But I promised those two men, Petey and Marv, that I'd keep myself hidden at the house. And…I don't know what your heart says to you. I was afraid." David looked down at his feet and twisted his cap in his hands like a medieval serf appearing before his aristocratic mistress.

Hiram cleared his throat again. "Well, I reckon I have chores to do over at the Brubaker mansion. The B&B, that is. I'd best be headed out."

David stepped aside as Hiram opened the door to leave. "You come on over to the B&B when you're ready, said Hiram, "and I'll drive you back to Jenkin's Hollow. Be strong and of good courage."

"Thank you, sir," With effort, David took his eyes off Serafina to address Hiram. "I believe you are my best friend in this village."

Serafina and David stood in silence for a few seconds after Hiram's departure. She had recovered some color in her face and struggled to regain her composure. She walked around behind the counter as if to shield herself from David's presence.

"Serafina, my love, you look more beautiful than ever. I've missed you so. Please, let me explain what happened. Will you let me?" David's dark eyes were intent on her face, but he hadn't moved since he stepped into the shop.

She looked down. Those eyes! They always bewitched her. Her heart flopped like a trapped bird in her chest.

"Well, come and sit," said Serafina pointing to an old ladderback chair next to the shelves. She tried to sound flippant, but failed.

"If I may, I would rather come and stand across from you, Serafina. I want to be near you, after all this time."

Serafina gulped. "Fine, then stand on the other side of the counter, I guess."

David walked over and laid his cap on the end of the massive old counter that had been repainted a bright purple by Serafina. He didn't speak, but continued to stare at her.

Serafina pretended to busy herself with the bags in front of her. She knew her body language betrayed her and she tried to steady her shaking hands. "Well, what's your story? Why didn't you come back to the camp?" Her voice picked up strength as she spoke. "You promised me you'd be back in three weeks, and I never saw you after that until today. Or until I glimpsed you in the window at Bessie's, that is. I waited for you for six months. Six months, David, with not a word from you." She was grateful to feel anger surging through her body, replacing the helpless tenderness she always experienced in David's presence.

"Serafina. I am sorry." The intensity of his emotions caused his accent to grow stronger. "I went back to Bucharest to finish up a deal I'd made with some business people there. I was selling them software for their computer systems."

"Software from where?" demanded Serafina sharply. "I assume you mean pirated software, don't you?"

David dropped his gaze. "Yes, this is so. The business people I was dealing with were part of the Romanian mafia. I did not know this when I started, you must believe me. They did not like what I delivered and demanded more. I spent the next eight months working to meet their demands, in fear of my life. I was afraid they would trace any contacts I made at the time. I did not want to put you in danger as well. I stayed hidden and was afraid to contact anyone."

Serafina had stopped packaging herbs and stared at David. "Another failed business project. Are they still looking for you? Is that really why you're here?"

"No, that deal is completed and I will not do another. In fact, I wish to work in the world of plants and gardens. My Romany heritage is full of knowledge about plants and herbs. But when I returned to camp and found you were gone…well, there was nothing left for me among my people anymore. You took my heart with you."

"I suppose you're here without proper papers?"

"I've overstayed my visa, yes, it's true. It took me so long to find you. But if you will come back to me, I'll return to Europe and get whatever papers I need. We can start a new life, Serafina, here in America or in Europe. If you will not return to me, I have no life anywhere."

David's eyes filled with tears as he spoke, and Serafina was alarmed. She'd seen him sad, but had never known him to cry, not even when their child was stillborn after four months of pregnancy.

"David. When I thought I saw you at Bessie's, all those feelings of being abandoned by you rushed back to me. Just like it felt when my father abandoned my mother and me when I was six. Then later I heard your violin playing our song, and I almost fell apart."

She leaned forward on the counter. "I never stopped loving you, David, but I don't know if I can trust you to stay by me after such a long absence. An absence without a single word. And how did you find me, anyway? I never told you about Custer's Mill. I wanted to leave it behind and never think about it again." She laughed. "But here we both are."

"It was a difficult task to find you. You never told me your last name. You took my name when we married, and said yours didn't matter anymore. But I found an old woman in another camp…the old fisherman's wife who doctored our people with herbs and remedies from the forests. She knew your name, I don't know how."

"You mean old Selina! Yes, a wonderful old lady, so wise. We talked for hours and hours after you went missing. And she taught me some of her craft, which Bessie continued to do when I returned. " Serafina's eyes became dreamy. "She always told me you were still alive and would find me one day."

"My love. You'll come back to me?" David's dark eyes held Serafina's.

"Well, I always told you we never had a proper American wedding, just a gypsy ceremony and party in the woods." She pulled herself to her full height and spoke primly. "I shall consider remarrying you in a proper wedding here in Custer's Mill. But until then, you stay at Bessie's and I'll keep my apartment."

David whooped loudly, flew around the counter and picked Serafina up by the waist. He swung her around, then they held each other in a long, tight embrace, tears of joy flowing down their faces.

Friday Night

May 31

By ten o'clock, the guests were in their rooms, packed and eager for their departure in the morning. The house was quiet except for the creaks and groans old houses always make on breezy nights. Emma wondered why creaks always seemed to be the loudest when it was dark. Of course, she strained her ears to hear any and every sound, especially the sound of feet on the stairs leading to the attic. She wondered if those two women would try to sneak back up there tonight. At least there was an officer on the porch.

She sat in the embroidered vanity chair and waited. After fifteen minutes, she was rewarded with the sound of a door creaking open and very faint steps. But the footsteps faded away. No one was headed for the attic, right now at least.

Emma turned off her lamp and opened the door of her room, peering down the stairway to the landing below. Nothing. She crept slowly down the stairs, careful to step on the outside of each riser to avoid squeaks. As she arrived on the second floor, she could see a light moving at the bottom of the main staircase. A flashlight, she thought. Who's sneaking around the house with a flashlight at this hour?

She continued down the stairs to the front hallway and kept to the shadows along the wall. A full moon helped light the way, but she wanted to remain invisible.

The night walker was in the kitchen now, and it sounded like the back door was opening. Was someone trying to get away? To leave during the night? Emma wanted to see where this person was heading before she alerted the officer who sat on the front porch. It would be embarrassing if someone was after a glass of milk or hot tea in the night. She slipped into the dining room and peeked around the corner of the sliding doors to the kitchen, just in time to see the door to the cellar close without a sound.

The cellar! Someone was headed to the cellar, either to hide or to escape. Maybe this night walker hoped to leave the house unseen through that door.

Emma crept across the kitchen floor and slowly opened the door to the cellar. She left it slightly ajar in case she needed to return quickly or silently. The rich, musty odor of the dirt floor and years of apple storage still lingered in the air. It rose up to meet her as she descended the rough board stairs. Faint moonlight through the dusty window-wells illuminated an old workbench with a row of glass jars of nails, screws and miscellany. Nails hammered into the wood above the bench held bundles of rope and a few old tools.

But no one was there. The light had vanished.

***

Jake was frustrated. He tapped his finger on the arm of his chair. What am I missing? Something important, for sure. The facts didn't add up. Andy Davis had motive and opportunity. So did his wife. And Martha Stanton had a romantic attachment to Wright years ago. Was she bitter?

And then there was that stranger, David Nicolescu. Was he connected to Frank Wright in any way, and they'd missed it? Questioning him earlier hadn't revealed anything to place him at the murder scene, but he had no alibi. Jake exhaled loudly.

He might as well go see what Dove had to report.

"Dove," said Jake, his voice sharper than he intended as he strode into the front office where Jason sat at his small green metal desk.

Jason looked up from his computer. "Sir?" Papers lay scattered around. The young man's eyes were rimmed with red and his hair was rumpled. It had been a very long day, and no rest was in sight for either man.

With effort, Jake moderated his tone. No use berating his overworked deputy. "What have you turned up on those items from the strongbox? Anything yet?"

"Well, I've just confirmed that those silver spoons and forks in the box are the same as the ones missing from the B&B," said Jason. "They match up exactly with the descriptions Nanette gave us."

Jason held up the photo of the old coins for Jake. "And there are the coins, too, sir. I'm checking out stolen antique coins as well."

"I want you to check on the jewelry we found in the box, Dove. Miss Fischer said they belonged to her late parents, but I wonder..."

"Right, sir, I'm on it."

"I'm going to start looking through the pictures I took of all the papers from that box," said Jake. "I'm not sure they're of any importance, but you never know. I'm determined to turn over every stone until we find something that makes sense and gets us going in the right direction. One thing I'm sure of, though. Someone in that B&B is a murderer."

Jason nodded, then turned his attention to his computer screen.

Back in his own office, Jake put the photos in a stack before he began to peruse them again, one by one. First, he took the time to jot down a quick note on his calendar reminding himself to contact his lawyer to update his will to include Professor Nelson and his soon-to-be new bride, Maria, as guardians for Kate.

He glanced at the old clock over the door. It was late. Another missed dinner with Kate. Another missed bedtime. When this was all over, he'd take her someplace special, just the two of them. Maybe go to Williamsburg for a long weekend, or to D.C. and the National Zoo. He'd let her pick.

***

Jason stared at the image of the emerald ring. He took a deep breath and hunkered down to the task at hand. He was no jewelry expert, but Chief Preston needed this information and needed it fast. He'd do his best.

After forty-five minutes of research, he sat back and jotted down several notes. If the stones were determined to be precious gems, the total value of the jewelry from the strongbox was well over $20,000. The emerald ring alone was worth a whopping $7,500. Jason gave a long, low whistle.

Next, he needed to determine if any of the jewelry was stolen or if it indeed belonged to the sisters, fair and square. Another thirty minutes passed before he found it: a police report that listed an emerald ring and several sets of earrings stolen in Richmond, Virginia, in February of this year. The case was still open, and the stolen items had not been retrieved. Total value was over $18,000.

He read further down the page of the report. Two suspects, Glenda and Isobel Fischer, were apprehended a day after the robbery, but later released for lack of evidence. Jason whooped again. He rushed down the hall and almost collided with Jake who was walking toward the conference room with a sheaf of papers in his hand.

"Dove, I've found something very interesting," said Jake.

"So have I, sir," said Jason, unable to wait to hear what his boss had to say. "It appears our two little old ladies may be jewelry thieves with the stolen property in their possession. You have to come see this police report from Richmond."

The two men hovered over the report on Jason's screen as Jake read the report. "Well, they're busted, Dove. Nice work. Looks like we now we have two crimes on our hands. Theft and murder. I need to contact the Richmond Police right away and let them know."

"I was coming to show you something I've found that gives them a motive to kill Frank Wright," said Jake." These are letters to the sisters from their brother, Wilhelm. He sent them while he was a Marine in Vietnam. Wilhelm mentions his commanding officer, First Lieutenant Wright. Look what else I found. Isn't this Frank Wright?" Jake handed Jason the copy of a newspaper article.

"I've seen this before." Jason looked at the document and then pulled a sheet of paper from under a stack of documents on the conference table. "These are the same articles. I looked at this several days ago, but once I realized it was Frank in the picture, I didn't bother to read the names of the other soldiers. It says here that Wilhelm Fischer was killed."

"Let's see if we can find anything else about Private Fischer." responded Jake.

Jason typed in the name and found an obituary for Private Wilhelm Fischer. He started to read.

"Private Wilhelm Fischer, was killed on March 27, 1973, in the line of duty in Saigon, Vietnam. He is preceded in death by his parents Ruppert and Wilomina Fischer of Richmond, Virginia. He is survived by his sisters Glenda Fischer and Isobel Fischer. His commanding officer, First Lieutenant Frank Wright, posthumously recommended him for the Purple Heart in honor of his bravery in action. He will be buried with full military honors in Arlington Cemetery."

"Does this mean that the sisters somehow blame Frank Wright for the death of their brother?" asked Jason. "But why? How did he die?"

"An interesting question, Dove. There's another article from the strongbox that gives us the answer. An article by none other than Martha Stanton, reporting on a truck accident on March 27, 1973, involving U.S. Marines. The driver of that truck was Frank Wright."

"That means this Wilhelm Fischer's death could be motive for the murder of Frank Wright," said Jason. "Over the years, his sisters, Glenda and Isobel, may have held a grudge against Wright. But we still have no murder weapon, sir, and no proof they had opportunity."

Both men jumped at the sound of the Jake's phone. It was late and the building was quiet.

He pulled his phone out of his pocket. "Preston here." He paused. "You did? How long ago? Stay in your cottage. We'll come right over and check it out."

"Come on, Dove. That was Hiram Steinbacher. Said he's seen 'creepers' in the cellar. We need to get over to the B&B. Make sure you have your weapon."

***

Emma peered under the stairs. There was a doorway into dark room that once held loads of coal poured down a chute from the side of the house. Had her night walker disappeared into that room?

Cautiously, she stepped around the stairs and pressed her back to the rough stone foundation wall. She had to be careful. She wasn't sure who or what was in the cellar. Suddenly, the door opened and a blinding beam of light shone directly into her eyes.

"Aha! It's you! The nosy Miss Library Lady." Isobel stepped out of the coal room and faced Emma. Glenda stood behind her, smiling.

"Well, I hate to be the one to tell you," said Isobel in a harsh whisper, "but you've made a fatal mistake. Now you must go the way of the illustrious Frank Wright. The celebrated army man who killed our brother."

Emma froze. Isobel walked toward her, a sharp, narrow knife in her hand. Her blue eyes held a fanatical gleam.

Isobel glanced at Glenda for a moment, then whispered again with unsettling, quiet rage. "Sister, now look what your interference has done. This wouldn't have happened if you'd left well enough alone and let me take care of that man myself."

Glenda's voice sounded strangely young and high-pitched, almost as if she were an angry child. Her forehead was creased and her lips set in a pout. "Oh, Isobel, how was I to know you planned to stab him that very night? I put a little antifreeze in the tea he was drinking at that picnic. That's much less messy than stabbing him. No blood at all. You didn't tell me what you were planning to do. You never let me do the fun things."

Isobel glared at her sister in silence and Glenda looked down at her feet.

Emma shivered with a chill brought on by more than the cool dampness of the cellar. These women were unbalanced. Was it possible to reason with at least one of them?

She decided to lodge an appeal with Glenda, whose face had resumed its typical kindly look. "Glenda, you don't want your sister to get in more trouble, do you? The police already know about your thefts. In fact, Jake was here this afternoon asking questions about you two, about things you took from this house. They'll be here any minute." Emma hoped it was true.

Glenda's look changed to regret. "I'm sorry, Miss, but you shouldn't have followed us down here. Now we have to kill you, right, sister? You know we only planned to kill one person, that reckless driver who killed our dear brother in Vietnam." She giggled and looked at Isobel. "And it looks like we killed him twice."

"Well that was your fault, Glenda, since I was already planning to kill him," said Isobel. "Now pay attention! If we kill Miss Nosy here, it won't look like we did it. We'll make it look like she fell down the stairs and fell on the knife that will have her fingerprints all over it. Now step over here, Miss, while I tie your hands. We're leaving tonight, and need to pack up a few articles in the coal room first. Glenda, put our things into Father's leather satchel while I tie up Miss Nosy. Put your hands behind your back." Isobel gestured with the knife.

Emma wondered if Isobel would put the knife down while she tied her wrists. Could she overtake her?

Isobel set the knife on a step and held Emma by the wrists. She was unnaturally strong, but Emma was able pull one hand free. Isobel grabbed the blade and held it against Emma's neck. "And now where are you going, lady? Glenda, tie up her wrists while I hold the knife at her lily-white throat."

Glenda smiled at Emma apologetically and proceeded to wrap some jute rope tightly around and around her wrists. It cut into her skin. "Now I'll go finish packing," she said. "Then we can toss her down the stairs. Really only a minor inconvenience to our plans, Sister. No need to get ruffled. But I do wish you'd let us keep that fancy knife we found," she added with a pout.

"I told you Glenda," said Isobel, "we had to put suspision on someone else. And that snooty woman deserved it."

Emma realized with horror that these two women were more than just unbalanced. They were crazy. There would be no reasoning with them. She squeezed her eyes shut and prayed for Jake to get here. A scrabbling sound near the window well gave her sudden hope. The outside cellar hatch door opened with a loud creak and Isobel stalked over to the bottom of the cement stairs. First Emma saw shoes and jeans, then Hiram Steinbacher's face appeared under the floor joists. He faced Isobel.

"What are you doing here, you lazy good-for-nothing? Get over there by Miss Nosy." She motioned with her knife.

Hiram looked at Emma and walked to her side. "Are you all right, Miss?" he asked, with uncharacteristic concern. "Have they hurt you?"

"I'm okay for now, Mr. Steinbacher. They plan to kill me, though, or so they say."

"That right? Well, thought I saw some light under the house. Wondered if there were creepers down here. Long time ago, Miss Bertha gave me the keys for the hatch. I reckoned it was time to use 'em. Been creepers in my shed, too. Don't like creepers. That officer on the porch didn't see a thing, I reckon."

"You two shut up now." Isobel's voice was tinged with hysteria. "No talking. You stand right there, Mister, hands behind your back. One false move and I'll cut your lady-friend's neck. Believe me, I will." Holding the cold blade against Emma's throat, she motioned to Glenda with her head. "Tie him up. Or wait! We can make it look like he killed her. Let me think. This might work fine."

While Isobel talked, Hiram felt along the wall behind him for the long piece of metal pipe he'd seen leaning against the old limestone foundation. He took a half step backward to reach it as Glenda gathered another length of rope from the old workbench.

Without a second's hesitation, he swung the pipe out in front of himself and caught Isobel behind the knees. She crumpled to the ground with a cry and the knife skittered across the dirt floor stopping next to Emma's feet. Emma put her foot on the handle as Glenda moved to retrieve it. Hiram held the pipe up and said, "I wouldn't do that, if I were you. If you do, this pipe will come down on your head."

"You idiot, get the knife!" Isobel shouted at her sister. "And help me get up. I think he's broken my leg. "She moaned and cupped her hands around her leg.

"Like I said, don't move. And I mean both of you." Hiram's lips were set and his eyes were bright. "I reckon the police will be here in a moment, given that I called them before I came down here. I figured 'in a multitude of counselors there is safety. If you count the police as counselors, that is."

Glenda looked back and forth between her sister and Hiram, and remained where she was. A smile still played on her lips.

Faintly at first, then louder, the sound of sirens approached.

Hiram kept the pipe raised above Glenda's head until footsteps thundered into the kitchen above, and Jake's voice called out, "Emma, Emma, where are you?"

"Down here, Jake. I'm okay. We're okay."

Jake was the first one down the steps followed by Jason and three county officers. As they tended to the suspects, Jake gathered Emma into his arms, tied wrists and all, tears of relief in his eyes.

"Sir," said Jason. "I think we've got our murder weapon." He pointed to the knife on the floor. "I'll bag it."

"Right, Dove," said Jake, as he loosened the ropes around Emma's wrists. He put his arm around her. "You're shaking, Emma. Are you really okay?

"Yes," said Emma. "Thanks to Hiram." Her teeth were chattering.

"No ma'am," said Hiram. "All thanks be to God."

Saturday

June 1

"Can you believe it? Another murder in Custer's Mill?" Jacob Craun cut a large chunk of chicken fried steak into several bite sized pieces and lined them up on his plate.

His friend, Laurence George, leaned back in his chair and studied the laminated menu at the Spare Change Diner. "We're not doing so hot in murders per capita, if that's what you mean."

"We're soon gonna have folks moving up to Northern Virginia to get away from small town crime."

"Maybe so." Laurence was unusually quiet which puzzled Jacob. Usually Custer's Mill bookstore owner was not shy about expressing his opinions about everything from the current price of seed potatoes to the Washington Redskins losing streak.

"Something wrong, Laurence?" Jacob had finished his steak and was now drenching a large baked potato in sour cream.

"Keep eating like that, Jacob, and I'll be visiting you at the Mill City hospital."

"Don't change the subject, Laurence. What's bothering you?"

Laurence pushed the menu aside and looked out past the diner into the blustery day outside. "I was just remembering that Alex was one of those statistics. My brother contributed to the growing murder rate."

Jacob rubbed his chin and stared down at his plate. "I'm sorry, man. I didn't think."

"No, it's okay. I need to move on. This off-and-on rainy weather puts me in a melancholy mood. And now another murder."

"More unsweetened tea?" Not waiting for an answer, the waitress refilled both glasses. "Figured out what you want yet, Mr. George?"

"How about the grilled chicken special? Coleslaw and corn on the side," said Laurence. "Could you make it carry-out for me, please? I'll be eating at the bookstore today."

"What you need," said Jacob, "is to find yourself a good woman. Give you some new, happy memories instead of shutting yourself away in your shop."

"You could be right,Jacob, but that's easier said than done."

A brisk breeze blew in as the door opened and the three owners of the Compass Rose Bed & Breakfast hurried inside. The men nodded as the ladies settled into an adjacent booth.

"I have never been so glad to see anyone leave in my life!" Nanette said, moving over to let Jane and Marguerite stack their purses in the empty space beside her.

"If I never see another suitcase, dirty towel, or disheveled bed, I'll be happy," added Jane.

"I can't believe our dear Emma put her life in danger again," said Marguerite. "It makes me shake to think of what could have happened to her if Hiram hadn't arrived in time."

"I guess it was technically Jake who stepped in to save them both," said Jane. "We all were in danger. Any one of us could have been threatened. Not a one of us was safe with those two irrational sisters in the house."

"Greetings, ladies." The waitress stacked three menus on the table and poured three glasses of water. "Special today is chicken fried steak, two sides, and a drink for $7.99. I'll be back to take your order in a few minutes."

"I don't know why I thought this would be easy," said Marguerite. "But I thought we'd worked out all of the bugs, anticipated all of the snags, and prepared for all of the glitches."

"Well, to be fair," said Jane, "there is no way we could have anticipated a murder."

"That's exactly right," said a voice at the table behind them.

"If it isn't Jacob Craun, my favorite paint consultant," said Nanette. "Where's your buddy going?"

"Laurence? Aw, he was in a blue funk. This new murder reminded him of Alex and he got himself all worked up. He got carry-out and is heading back to the bookstore. Says being around all of those books comforts him." Jacob shook his head. "To each his own, I guess."

"Join us, Jacob," said Marguerite patting the seat beside her.

"Why, thank you ma'am. Jacob picked up his food and slid into the ladies' booth.

"How's things down at the hardware store?" asked Nanette.

"Better since you haven't been around for a while. Nobody fusses about my paint colors or gripes about my customer service."

"You know you miss me." Nanette grinned.

"Like poison ivy," Jacob grunted. "By the way, I take it that running a B&B was not quite as easy as you thought it was going to be."

"That's not fair, Jacob," said Marguerite. "A murder was more than we bargained for. A lot more."

The waitress came back to the table and stood, pen poised.

"We'll take three specials," said Nanette, speaking for the group. Cole slaw and broccoli for all three sides. We'll make it easy for you today."

"I just serve, Ms. Steele. You can order roasted hippo for all I care!"

"Heard it was two little old ladies who did him in," said Jacob.

"Well you heard right for a change. No idle rumors there. One stabbed him and one poisoned him. Double murder."

Jacob shook his head. "If you're not safe in Custer's Mill, where can you be safe?"

"Who's not safe?" Former town manager Billy Brubaker clapped Jacob on the shoulder and nodded to the three ladies. "From what I'm hearing, nobody's safe. Crazy murderers around every corner. Behind every bush."

Jacob shook his head. "Know what you mean, Billy. The wild west all over again."

"I do regret that he was murdered," said Billy. "But I'm not at all surprised somebody did him in. He really rubbed me the wrong way when I had to drive his tour group all over the place. Seemed to have his nose in everybody's business, including mine. If you ask me, that whole group was a piece of work. My Aunt Bertha would never have wanted them staying at her mansion." Billy shook his head.

"We weren't expecting such a troubled lot," said Jane.

"My point exactly," said Billy. "If you'd left my Aunt Bertha's house the way it was and hadn't turned it into a showplace this never would have happened." Billy slammed some change on the counter and stalked out the door just as Hiram was coming in.

"Ah, our town hero!" Nanette motioned Hiram to their booth.

Hiram walked slowly toward the group, twisting his grimy cap in both hands. "No glory belongs to me."

"Aw, don't be so modest, Hiram. You kept those crazy, murderous women at bay until the police came. You saved our Emma's life."

"And I'm eternally grateful," said Emma coming up behind Hiram.

"Good grief, is all of Custer's Mill gathering at the Spare Change Diner today?" said Jacob. He pulled a chair up to allow Emma a place at the table.

"Young lady, what are you doing out and about? You should be home in bed after all you went through yesterday." Marguerite shook her head in disbelief.

"What are you talking about? I wasn't hurt. There's not a scratch on me, just some chafed wrists. And why in the world would I stay in bed? I have work to do. In fact, I stopped by on my break to ask you ladies a few questions."

"Please, not about the murder," Jane began.

"No, not about the murder. About Serafina. Somebody said there's a rumor around town about her having a husband? "Emma looked incredulous.

Nanette shook her head. "Just idle gossip. Some people don't have enough to do. They have to make up bizarre stories about stuff they don't know anything about."

"You shall know the truth, and the truth will set you free." Hiram spoke in a low voice from the counter nearby.

"What are you saying, Hiram?" Emma stood up and joined him at the counter. "Do you mean to tell me that Serafina does have a husband?"

Hiram nodded slowly. The waitress handed him his order in a white paper bag. "Thank you. Here's ten dollars. You keep the change." Hiram, headed for the door.

"Wait," called Emma, "you can't quote a mysterious Bible verse like that and leave!" But Hiram was already outside.

"That man is so infuriating!" Emma shook her head. "If you don't know anything about the Serafina rumors, I'll head on over to the library. Somebody there is bound to have heard something."

"Don't go around listening to gossip," said Nanette. "I know Serafina pretty well. She didn't act like anything had changed when she came back to Custer's Mill. In fact, she sort of took up where she left off before she moved away."

"She flirted enough with Jake," said Emma. "Not very becoming of a married woman."

"What, you jealous?" asked Nanette, who was rewarded with an offended look from Emma.

"Doesn't sound legit to me, "added Jacob. "Has anyone asked Serafina about this? Seems to me the young lady has established herself and won't be moving anywhere.

"She's put heart and soul into her Serendipity Tea Shop," said Jane. "It's such a cozy little place. And Laurence mentioned she'd signed a two-year lease with him for the shop. Doesn't sound to me like she has plans to leave any time soon."

***

"Hey, Mr. Steinbacher! Wait up!" Emma had followed Hiram out of the diner and ran to catch up with him. Hiram slowed and let her walk beside him.

"I wanted to thank you for your part in my rescue, Mr. Steinbacher. If you hadn't suspected something was amiss, I might not be here today."

Hiram grunted.

"So," continued Emma, "I'd like to do something to show my appreciation to you. I know you're not one who likes to get too far away from the Brubaker place, but maybe I could take you to dinner at the new Italian place in Mill City. Jake and I went there a while back, and the food is delicious."

Hiram shook his head. "Too spicy."

"But you can get non-spicy food there too," protested Emma.

Again, Hiram shook his head.

"Well how about I treat you to a meal at the Spare Change Diner, then? I know you like to eat there."

"It's American food," was Hiram's only reply.

"I'll treat you to dinner at the diner, then. When would you like to go?"

"Not necessary," said Hiram.

"I know it's not necessary, Hiram. But I want to do something for you. You saved my life."

"I'll eat at the diner," said Hiram, increasing his pace. Emma had to walk fast to keep up with him.

"Then I'll get you a gift card, and then you can go when it's convenient for you. And Mr. Steinbacher, can you please slow down? I'd like to ask you one more question."

Hiram let her catch up again.

"What's that you said about Serafina? About the truth? Do you mean that she is married to that tall, dark man? Are the rumors more than rumors?"

"You shall know the truth, and the truth shall set you free."

"But that's what you said in the diner," said Emma. "What do you mean?"

But Hiram had already walked past her and this time she didn't try to keep up.

***

"What's the occasion? You actually came through the front door during regular business hours?" Emma pushed a pile of books out of the way and motioned for Serafina to put her library book in the open space.

"I guess that's fair enough," said Serafina, as she dropped the book on the desk. "I'm glad Bessie didn't read this travesty of herbal remedies," she said, pointing to the returned volume. "It's a collection of misinformation."

"I don't write 'em, Serafina. I just make them available for the public to criticize."

"Let me say that you should pull that one off the shelves. It's rubbish."

"Perhaps," agreed Emma. "So, Serafina, do you have a minute to talk?"

Serafina nodded. "Only a minute. I have to get back to the shop. I can't leave the 'back in a minute' sign up for hours."

Emma motioned for Serafina to follow her to the back office.

"What's up?" asked Serafina, looking puzzled as Emma closed the door.

"You know what's up," said Emma. "What's this I hear about you entertaining a handsome stranger?"

"Entertaining? Now isn't that an old-fashioned word. Certainly, you can do better than that, Emma!"

Emma bit her lip to hold back a sarcastic reply. "Come on, Serafina. Who is the tall, dark, handsome stranger I keep hearing about?"

Serafina moved over to the office window and looked out over Main Street. She waited a long minute before she said anything. When she finally spoke, her voice was soft. "His name is David. David Nicolescu. And he's my husband."

Emma stepped back. "So, the rumors are true? You are married?"

Serafina nodded.

"How long? When? Where?"

"One question at a time, Emma. Remember when I left school right after…?" Her voice trailed off.

"After Eric died in the fire. Yeah. I remember. Probably not an event

I'm likely to forget."

"I'm truly sorry, Emma."

Emma tried not to react. This was the first time Serafina had even come close to expressing regret for all that had happened in the past.

Serafina continued. "Anyway, right after the fire, I had to get away. I scraped together my savings and hopped on a plane to Europe. To Southeastern Europe. To Romania."

Emma nodded. "Go on."

"Well, I had used up all of my money on the trip there. I was broke and had no place to stay. So, I did what any decent free-spirit would do. I joined a gypsy caravan!"

"You did what?" Emma's voice rose an octave.

"Just hear me out, Ms. Librarian. Listen to the rest of my story. Turns out, the clan was a musical group and they appreciated my high soprano. They took me on as part of their act. Two days later, I met David. And the rest, as they say, is history."

"But it's not history," said Emma. "You ended up back in Custer's Mill and this David— where did he go?"

"It's a long and winding story, Emma. Someday I'll tell you about it. But right now, suffice it to say, he's back. And I have a feeling we'll never let an ocean separate us again."

Epilogue

Saturday, June 16

Emma closed her eyes and inhaled the sweet scent of roses. The ladies had outdone themselves with decorations. How did those three find time to do the things they managed to accomplish? Hiram probably cut the roses. She could picture him snipping the best and brightest of Bertha's roses. Each pew held a spray of large, peachy-pink blooms tied together with pink satin ribbon. The archway at the front of the church was covered in tiny white lights, and the bride's bouquet was a stunning mix of baby's breath and roses. Bertha would be so pleased. Emma moved a step closer to her Aunt Mia and touched her elbow lightly. The ceremony was about to begin.

Jake stood beside Uncle Albert. Emma stifled a smile. The unflappable, self-possessed police chief was nervous. He shifted from one foot to the other and straightened his tie. Their eyes met for a brief moment and Emma winked. Jake smiled and winked back.

Emma was thrilled that her dad had agreed to walk his sister, Mia, down the aisle. He stood with the other participants in back of the sanctuary, waiting to play his part in the ceremony. He'd scrubbed all traces of engine grease from his fingernails and had trimmed his scraggly beard to a neat point. He looked quite handsome and Emma felt proud to be his daughter.

The small church was almost full and conversation hummed quietly along with the prelude music. Emma's brother, Josh, and her sister-in-law, Shirley, sat on the front pew.

Across the aisle on the front row of the groom's side, Kate sat between Nanette and Marguerite, with Jane and Terri at the end of row. The ladies were insistent that they sit with Kate, Albert's only living relative, to serve as his adopted family.

As Nanette had predicted, the whole town had turned out for this wedding. Marv and Petey Blue returned to town just in time to hear all the news of Frank Wright's murder and Emma's near disaster. Hoyt Miller and Lawrence George sat together. Billy slid into the back pew. Hiram sat with Sissy and her boys. Lula Parker stood up, ready to sing her solo accompanied by Reba Dove on the piano.

Serafina and the dark-haired man sat together, their arms entwined. Rumors were running around town that this was Serafina's husband and that they had met in Europe. It was even said that he was a gypsy and that he was hiding from the mafia.

Emma found it hard to believe that her one-time best friend would have kept such a secret. True, their relationship was strained. Also, true, Serafina got under her skin. But would her oldest friend end up leaving Custer's Mill with the handsome stranger? Emma was surprised at the sadness she felt at such a thought.

At last, Reverend Winston welcomed the guests and the ceremony began.

***

Hiram stood along the curve of the driveway. His arms were in constant motion as he directed cars into the provisional parking spots along the rose hedge. The line of various vehicles…trucks, sedans, and minivans… stretched for as far as he could see. People piled out of the cars and made their way into the Compass Rose Bed & Breakfast.

"Great day for a party, Hiram." Billy stood next to Hiram. "From the looks of it, the whole town's come out for this."

"Feed them and they will come," Hiram grumbled. He threw his up his hand to stop the next car. He motioned for them to start another row down the hill.

"I'd say we have as many curiosity seekers as we do well wishers for the new couple," said Billy. "Custer's Mill folks don't need much of a reason to celebrate. Heard the ladies were making my Aunt Bertha's tea cakes. My favorite, you know. I'd better get inside before they're all gone."

Billy left Hiram to his task. The people kept coming. It was true. Custer's Mill folks liked a good party and any excuse to be in the Brubaker mansion. For decades this home and the Brubaker family had been part of the town's history, but access to the house had been by invitation only. The ladies had changed all of that with Bertha's generous gift. Marguerite, Jane and Nanette had opened the doors of the Brubaker mansion for all to enjoy. The people were grateful. And curious.

***

Marguerite watched as Terri and Jane put two large trays of tea sandwiches on the dining room table. They'd hardly had time to get home from the service before folks started arriving. Word had spread quickly of the marriage of Maria and Albert, and a big crowd was turning out to help them celebrate.

"Thank goodness we did most of the preparation before we left for church," said Jane.

"I've held my breath hoping people wouldn't show up with crock-pots again," added Nanette. "After Bessie's funeral, I'd be glad to never see another pot with squirrel meat and gravy."

"I think we learned our lesson. This time we let people know all food would be provided by the Compass Rose Bed & Breakfast."

Marguerite and Terri welcomed the guests from the front foyer. They ushered them into the parlor where the bride and groom were seated. The table was set up buffet style with piles of food—chicken salad sandwiche and ham biscuits, a selection of cheeses and crackers, and several other trays of finger foods. A tall, elaborate wedding cake sat in the center of the buffet surrounded by a variety of pastries, including cream puffs, cookies, and a large platter of Bertha's famous tea cakes. Billy had already piled his plate high with his aunt's beloved treats.

Terri and Lawrence George came in together. No one seemed to notice the couple except Jane who welcomed them into the room.

Guests encircled the new bride and groom, leaving no room for the wedding party. Jake and Emma stood along the side of the parlor and were joined by Marv and Petey Blue.

"Chief, I guess we missed some big goin's-on while we were on the other side of the mountain," said Petey Blue. Marv nodded.

Not wanting to discuss the recent events of Frank's murder and Emma's close call, Jake tried to steer the conversation in another direction. "If you mean Mia and Albert's wedding, I'd say you got back right in time.

"Aw, now, we hear you saved Miss Emma again...along with the help of Hiram."

"Yes, they did," said Emma. She leaned into Jake, and he put his arm around her. "Glad you two made it back in time to help my aunt and uncle celebrate."

"So are we," said Petey Blue. "I've been hearin' there may be another marriage we should celebrate. Marv and I had no idea when we let that foreigner stay at Bessie's that he knew Serafina."

"Yeah, I want to talk to you about that," said Jake. "What were you thinking when you let a stranger stay at Bessie's? Don't you think it would have been a good idea to let me know he was there?"

Before Petey Blue could answer, Sissy came up beside Emma and Jake. "May I take Emma away for a minute? We've got something to talk about." Sissy didn't wait for an answer. She pulled Emma by the arm. "Come on. We need to talk to Serafina, she's over there by the window."

"Serafina, how could you not tell us?" asked Sissy. "Growing up, the three of us used to tell each other everything, no secrets. Then you two went away to college and I got married. And now, here we are."

Serafina's face flushed slightly. "Times change, Sissy. And I didn't think it was worth telling. David disappeared without a word, and I thought it was over. Besides it was a Roma marriage, maybe not legal in the U.S."

Emma looked at her friend. "But you were husband and wife. Don't you think we'd want to know that you had a husband?" she said.

Before Serafina could answer, Mia announced to the group that she was ready to toss the bouquet. All single women were called to the center of the room.

"Well, go ahead, both of you," insisted Sissy. "If you're not sure your marriage is legal yet, Serafina, then you need to get in there. Go, go." Sissy shooed her two friends into the small crowd of women who had gathered. Serafina and Sissy reluctantly joined at the back of the group.

"Here we go!" Mia's back was to the young women, some who anxiously waited and hoped they would catch the spray of roses. Albert stood near his bride, a look of pure joy and happiness on his face.

Mia started to count. The guests joined her. "One...two...three."

The toss was high and the bouquet sailed over raised arms. A few petals came raining down. Serafina and Emma kept their arms at their sides, each waiting to see if the other would try to make the catch. They looked at each other and shrugged as it came to rest at their feet.

Kate Preston dashed from the side of the group and grabbed the spray. "Look, Sam, I got the bouquet," said Kate, as she waved the flowers above her head. "Hey, let's go outside and play wedding," she said.

Sam nodded and ran after her.

David arrived at Serafina's side and she took his hand. "Why did you not catch those beautiful flowers?" he said. "It is your custom, yes? Serafina, I have decided. We will get married your way. I like this American wedding style."

Serafina smiled and melted into the muscular arm he draped over her shoulder. The pair walked outside onto the porch, present only to each other.

Emma's and Sissy's mouths dropped. They stood still and watched their friend be swept away by the handsome dark stranger. They'd never before seen a man who could wrap Serafina around his little finger.

"Excuse me, ladies." Jake had come to stand next to the two friends. "Emma, may I speak to you?" Without waiting for an answer, Jake took Emma's arm and gently guided her to a quiet corner of the room. "I thought maybe you'd catch the bouquet, Emma."

Emma laughed. "I was waiting for Serafina to catch it, and I guess she was waiting for me. So, your Kate made off with it, and she's welcome to it. But it's obvious Serafina and David are in love and will be getting married officially. And settling here in Custer's Mill, I hope."

"Emma, I'm hoping you'll agree that the time is right for us...for you and me...to start really working on our relationship. See where it leads us."

Emma gulped and tried to hide her instant nervousness. "You mean like regular dating? A boyfriend-girlfriend relationship?"

"Yes, precisely," said Jake. "Be honest. Don't tell me you can't feel the attraction between us. Your hands are shaking."

"Yes, they are," said Emma. "Nerves. You need to understand that this is hard for me. But you're right." She held out her hand and he squeezed it gently. She took a deep breath. "Jake Preston, I'd be honored to be your girlfriend. Let the relationship begin. No promises, though. At least not yet," she added.

"Deal," he said, and slid his arm around her waist.

***

"I'd say our reception was a success." Jane picked up the tray where Bertha's tea cakes had been. Only crumbs remained. "We must have had over a hundred people come to wish the newlyweds well."

Terri cleared the last of the trays from the dining room table when she paused. "Ladies, as your financial adviser and as a part of this family, I've observed that you're the happiest when entertaining the folks of Custer's Mill. Maybe we need to rethink this bed & breakfast idea." She retreated to the kitchen to clean up the rest of the dishes.

"She's right, our first experience with having overnight guests was a disaster," said Jane.

"Who could have known what those sisters had cooked up? It'll be better next time," assured Marguerite.

"I'm not sure I want a next time," said Nanette. "Maybe we should go back to the tea room idea."

"But you know Bertha wasn't a quitter," said Jane. "We need to keep the faith, my friends. If she could see us now, Bertha would want us to keep going."

The long drapes fluttered at the bay window in the parlor, and a fragrant breeze floated over the room.

***

The sun set reluctantly, almost as if it hated to see the day end. The sky, first streaked with cantaloupe orange, faded quickly to coral pink, and then to pale yellow. When at last all traces of light disappeared from the horizon, the earth seemed to sigh and settle in for a long night's rest.

Custer's Mill had been a flurry of activity today. Mia and Albert's wedding pulled the town together for a much-needed reunion. Neighbors caught up on news, farmers discussed late spring planting, and even the long dormant garden club members had agreed to hold a meeting at the end of June.

Somewhere in the garden behind mansion the old matriarch watched the house lights go out one by one. Her sigh was wistful but not sad. Once she was at the hub of activity in her little town. Now, she was content to observe from a different perspective. In the grand scheme of things, time was an illusion. Not everybody knew that, of course. She didn't expect them too. No more than she expected them to believe she still watched over Custer's Mill. But she enjoyed keeping an eye on the comings and goings of the place whether or not anyone knew she was there.

At the end of the garden, near the wood's edge, she saw another figure walking, occasionally bending down as though picking a flower or a long blade of grass. Oh yes. That Appalachian woman was here now. They had next to nothing in common, but they were both here to muse, to ponder, and to remember.

Mary Fulk Larson is...

- Mary M. Smith, Ed.D., who enjoyed a thirty-year career as a public school teacher, university professor, and curriculum developer, and now volunteers for community and church organizations.

- Tammy Fulk Cullers, M.A. Ed., who publishes a small newspaper, enjoys acting in community theatre, and teaches middle school English

- Barbara Larson Finnegan, M.B.A., master gardener, neophyte farmer, and small business owner.

Collectively, the authors have ten grown children and twelve grandchildren, and live with their husbands in the lovely Shenandoah Valley.

Made in the USA
Middletown, DE
29 October 2022